THE FIRST FENCE . . .

"All right, Lisa—let's go," Max called out.

Despite her resolve, Lisa looked at the course and felt her heart begin hammering even faster. She couldn't ride this course. The jumps were enormous. What was she thinking, asking to ride Samson in the Macrae?

Suddenly Lisa sat up straighter in the saddle and took up the reins firmly. *Max wouldn't let you ride in the Macrae Valley Open if he thought you were going to completely fail. I mean,* she corrected herself, *Max must have confidence in you to let you ride in the Macrae. He must feel you have a chance.*

She looked straight ahead at Samson's ears, which were pricked up eagerly for her signal to start. Confidence, Lisa knew, was a huge part of jumping. Determinedly she shortened the reins and cantered Samson in a circle. They broke out of the circle and headed for the first fence.

THE SADDLE CLUB

SHOW JUMPER

BONNIE BRYANT

A SKYLARK BOOK
NEW YORK • TORONTO • LONDON • SYDNEY • AUCKLAND

RL 5, 009–012

SHOW JUMPER

A Bantam Skylark Book / May 1999

ISBN 0-553-48672-1

Published simultaneously in the United States and Canada.

Bantam Books are published by Bantam Books, a division of Random House, Inc. Its
trademark, consisting of the words "Bantam Books" and the portrayal of a rooster, is
Registered in U.S. Patent and Trademark Office and in other countries. Marca
Registrada. Bantam Books, 1540 Broadway, New York, New York 10036.

PRINTED IN THE UNITED STATES OF AMERICA

OPM   0 9 8 7 6 5 4 3 2 1

*I would like to express my special thanks
to Minna Jung for her
help in the writing of this book.*

THE SUN SHONE brightly in a clear blue sky. A scattering of applause died down after the awarding of the second-place ribbon. A dramatic hush fell over the crowd as everyone waited for the announcement of the blue-ribbon winner.

Lisa Atwood, waiting near the entrance of the ring on Samson, felt a nervous flutter in her stomach. Even though she already knew what was coming next, she still couldn't quite believe what had just happened. In fact, she couldn't believe that she was even there, let alone about to experience the next moment.

Standing at the judges' desk in their box, a stately, gray-haired man held up a microphone, and the loud-speakers blared. "I am pleased to announce the winner of today's junior jumping division," he said solemnly.

"This poised young rider gave a spectacular performance on a spectacular horse. I'm sure you were all as thrilled as I was to see this young lady take these fences on what is, in my opinion, one of the most promising horses we've seen in a long time."

He held up a silver cup and smiled broadly. "The blue ribbon and challenge trophy for junior jumping goes to Lisa Atwood, riding Samson from Pine Hollow Stables!"

The crowd broke into loud applause. When she heard it, Lisa's nervousness vanished. Suddenly she felt a tremendous surge of excitement and happiness. They were clapping for her! And, of course, for Samson, the best jumper she had ever ridden. She gently urged the black gelding into the ring and rode toward the judges to accept the trophy and the blue ribbon. Samson seemed to understand that he had performed well and that this was an extra-special occasion. He picked up his feet briskly and tossed his mane several times.

As she and Samson made their way to the judges' box, Lisa searched the crowd. Although she was almost too excited to focus, she wanted to share this moment with several very important people. After scanning the blur of faces, she finally glimpsed her mother and her two best friends, Carole Hanson and Stevie Lake. All three were clapping madly, and both Carole and Stevie were giving her a huge V sign for victory. Lisa grinned and waved at them.

2

Then she caught a glimpse of Max Regnery III, the owner of Pine Hollow, sitting with his mother. She was Pine Hollow's stable manager and universally known as Mrs. Reg. Max also owned Samson. Lisa was accustomed to seeing Max every week as her occasionally stern, always professional riding instructor, but now all his normal restraint was gone. He had a huge smile on his face, and he and Mrs. Reg were clapping like crazy.

As the applause grew even louder, Samson began to get a little bothered by the noise. Without warning, he pulled sideways with little, jerky steps. Lisa acted quickly, taking firmer hold of the reins and leaning forward so that Samson could hear her over the noise. "Easy, Samson—nothing to get worried about, just a little applause for you," she said gently. She tightened the reins to maintain light contact with his mouth and urged him to walk a little more quickly toward the judges' box. Immediately Samson calmed down.

Then Lisa reached the box, and a judge leaned over to pin the blue ribbon on Samson's bridle. The man with the microphone handed Lisa the silver cup. "Congratulations, Ms. Atwood," he said, shaking her hand. Lisa thanked him; then she and Samson joined the other competitors in the center of the ring.

As another round of applause began for the junior jumpers, Lisa leaned forward and patted Samson's neck. "We did it, boy!" she whispered to him. "We won!"

* * *

"LISA! WHERE ARE you? It's time to go!"

Her mother's voice shattered Lisa's thoughts and she jumped. The crowd and the applause melted away and she blinked, looking around her in a daze. She recognized her neatly made bed, the horse posters, and the books that lined the walls. She was in her bedroom, sitting at her desk—exactly the same spot where she had been fifteen minutes before, when she had started daydreaming.

But what a daydream! She had imagined winning the blue ribbon at the Macrae Valley Open. And as she slowly came back to reality, she knew that it was Wednesday morning, and that the *real* Macrae Valley Open was only two days away. It was one of the biggest horse shows on the A-rated show circuit, and she, Lisa Atwood, was going to be competing in the junior jumping division.

Carole and Stevie were also going to the Macrae Valley Open, which made Lisa all the more excited. Without her best friends there, she would have felt lost at the Macrae. Since the three girls had met and formed The Saddle Club, they had gone through many adventures together: They had rescued horses from danger, met movie stars, and gone out West to ride at a dude ranch. Throughout these experiences, the girls had been brought even closer to each other and had won lots of friends by sticking to the two rules of The

4

Saddle Club. First, Saddle Club members had to be crazy about horses. Second, Saddle Club members had to be willing to help each other out.

Several weeks before, the prospect of going to the Macrae Valley Open had really put the two rules to the test. The girls, of course, were already familiar with the Macrae, one of the most famous horse shows in the country. The bad news was that Veronica diAngelo, The Saddle Club's worst enemy, was also entered in the competition, and worse yet, she was bragging to everyone at Pine Hollow that she would win the junior jumping division. Veronica was the laziest, most spoiled member of the girls' Pony Club, Horse Wise. With her parents' wealth and her champion jumper, Danny, Veronica had managed to persuade Max to enter her in the Macrae and transport Danny there in the Pine Hollow horse trailer—with an extra stall reserved for her equipment.

When they had heard this news—and gotten a dose of Veronica's bragging—The Saddle Club had put their heads together and acted quickly and decisively. Not only did the three girls want very badly to compete in the Macrae Valley Open, they also didn't want Veronica to be the only representative of Pine Hollow at the show and possibly—their worst nightmare—win the junior jumping event. So they hatched a plan to convince Max to take them along to the Macrae.

The first part of the plan had been simple in theory, painful in practice. Without any urging from Max, Carole, Lisa, and Stevie decided to show that they were completely indispensable. They had started spending hours and hours at Pine Hollow, doing stable chores and trying to help out in any way they could. Max had really welcomed their help because Red O'Malley, the head stable hand and himself an accomplished rider, had taken two weeks off to attend a riding clinic with a famous instructor. During his absence, The Saddle Club had pitched in to help run the stable. Mucking out stalls, cleaning tack, sweeping floors—"No job too small or too grimy!" Carole had joked during one particularly exhausting day. Max loved a well-run, clean stable and believed that every good rider should put in his or her share of stable work. Only Veronica, backed by her father's money and influence, managed to find some way to avoid helping out.

"You know, if Veronica put as much effort into doing work as she puts into getting out of it, she'd really accomplish something!" Stevie remarked one day. Her friends agreed, but it was obvious to everyone that Veronica was never going to change.

The other part of the campaign was trickier, especially since Pine Hollow was a tight-knit stable and everyone usually knew what everyone else was doing. The Saddle Club began to train Samson secretly to get him ready for the junior jumping division at the

Macrae Valley Open—the same division that Veronica had entered. The three girls had all been active in Samson's early training, because he'd been born at Pine Hollow (with their help) and they'd always had a special bond with the coal black gelding. Lisa had been the first to discover Samson's astounding natural jumping ability while exercising him as part of the group's stable chores.

The three girls were desperate for Samson to go to the Macrae. But as they spent more time training him and his talent became more and more obvious, Lisa began to worry: If Max *did* want Samson to go the Macrae Valley Open, who was going to ride him? Carole was definitely the most experienced member of the group, and Lisa fretted that Max would pick Carole to ride the gelding for the Open.

Additionally, Lisa had thought that Carole might have wanted to be the one to ride the young horse in his first competition. After all, it was Carole who had been especially fond of Cobalt, Samson's sire. Cobalt had been a beautiful, noble horse and an outstanding jumper. Carole, who had had no horse of her own at the time, had often volunteered to exercise and take care of the stallion when Veronica, who actually owned him, showed any disinclination to do so. As a result, Carole had loved the horse deeply—and had been devastated by his death after Veronica rode him carelessly over a dangerous jump.

Shortly after Cobalt's death, Samson had been born. His dam was Delilah, a palomino mare from Pine Hollow. Carole had also eventually acquired her own horse, Starlight—a bay gelding with a playful, gentle disposition, lively gaits, and a natural flair for jumping. Carole was so devoted to Starlight, it was almost unthinkable that she would ride another horse in a competition. Despite this, however, Lisa had still worried that Max would try to persuade Carole to ride Samson in the Macrae when he found out about the gelding's ability.

But by the time Max had finally learned of Samson's talent, Carole had already figured out what to do about the Macrae. First the three girls convinced him that Samson ought to compete in the big horse show. Then Carole argued that Lisa should be the one to ride the black horse, because she was the first to discover his talent. After watching Lisa ride over a jump course, and after hearing The Saddle Club's persuasive arguments, Max finally agreed to let Lisa ride Samson at the show. Stevie volunteered to be the tack manager and Carole took the last slot in Max's trailer with Starlight.

Thinking about the Macrae, now only two days away, Lisa picked up a pencil and began to chew the end nervously. "I'm going to do well," she said out loud, as if trying to convince herself. "I have a great horse."

Carole, Lisa believed, would definitely turn in a good performance—Starlight was a talented horse, and Carole was a skilled rider. But Lisa had never participated in such a major show before, and the Macrae Valley Open attracted the top riders from all over the country. Carole had already regaled Lisa and Stevie with stories of how fancy the Open was—the beautiful stables, the gourmet food served in the concession tents, and how unpleasantly snooty some of the competitors could be. Lisa couldn't even imagine how high the fences were going to be. *What if they've decided to raise them higher than ever this year?* she began to worry. *What if*—

"Lisa!" Her mother stood in the doorway of her bedroom, her hands on her hips and an exasperated expression on her face. "I've called you three times! If you don't hurry, we won't have time to get to the tack shop before your lesson begins."

Lisa scrambled up from her chair. "Sorry," she said sheepishly. As Mrs. Atwood shook her head resignedly and disappeared downstairs, Lisa glanced at the clock on her bedroom wall and then began grabbing her riding things. She had been thinking so hard about the Macrae, she hadn't even noticed the time. If Carole and Stevie had been there, they would have been shocked. Normally Lisa was the most punctual and organized member of The Saddle Club.

But if she had shared her thoughts with her friends, they would have understood. The Macrae was an important event, and besides, Carole and Stevie knew that Lisa, in addition to being punctual and organized, was also the biggest worrier of the group. "That's why you get good grades at school and I get graded on just keeping my head above water!" Stevie had said once.

Lisa quickly changed into her old breeches and a shirt. After gathering her boots and the rest of her riding gear, she ran out the door to join her mother.

Mrs. Atwood was already sitting behind the wheel of her car. She smiled at Lisa as she scrambled into the passenger seat. Her impatience had vanished, and Lisa suspected she knew why. For the past few weeks, her mother had been on cloud nine after learning that her daughter was going to ride in the Macrae Valley Open. Mrs. Atwood, who yearned to mingle with the "right" sorts of people in society, knew that the Macrae, held just outside Philadelphia's most exclusive neighborhoods, was one of the area's biggest society events.

Mrs. Atwood pulled out of the driveway and began heading toward the tack shop near Pine Hollow. "Are you excited about your new riding outfit?" she asked, leaning over and patting Lisa on the arm.

Lisa nodded, still out of breath from her dash down the stairs and into the car. Her mother had insisted on buying her a whole new riding outfit—boots, breeches, jacket, shirt. In fact, she had had to make the offer several times, because Lisa couldn't believe at first that her mother wanted to be so generous about anything to do with riding. Although Mrs. Atwood had originally signed Lisa up for riding lessons as part of her education in becoming "a young lady," she had been dismayed at the extent of Lisa's horse-craziness. All Lisa's other lessons—ballet, piano, needlepoint—had taken a backseat to her love of riding. But the fact that Lisa was riding in the *Macrae Valley Open*, an event that registered on her mother's society radar, made all the difference in Mrs. Atwood's attitude.

"I saw the most darling jacket in a catalog yesterday," Mrs. Atwood continued gushingly. "It was navy blue, which I think will be just right with your fair skin. Perhaps I'd better take you for a makeover at my beauty salon. You can get some new blusher and lip gloss. You don't want to look too pale for the show, do you?"

At any other time, Lisa would have winced and then good-humoredly persuaded her mother not to get her a makeover appointment. Lisa always tried to limit her involvement in activities that her mother thought would develop her "feminine qualities." Past experience had taught her that any activities planned by her mother could take away precious time from riding.

As her mother happily chattered about the Macrae, Lisa absently mumbled, "Sure, Mom," at regular intervals and continued to gaze out the car window. Within seconds she was daydreaming about the show again— but from a very different angle than her mother.

The girls had worked hard to convince Max to enter

Samson in the show because they all believed that the black horse deserved his first chance at a big event. But they also wanted Samson or Starlight to beat Veronica in the junior jumping division. The victory would be all the sweeter if Veronica had no idea what she was up against. Although Veronica respected Carole's experience as a rider, she had belittled Lisa's riding ability on more than one occasion, because Lisa hadn't been riding as long as Carole, Stevie, or Veronica.

Now, remembering the times that Veronica had made fun of her, Lisa felt a little wicked thrill of satisfaction. *Veronica has no clue about Samson*, she said to herself. *She probably thinks I'm riding Prancer, and that I'm just doing the show for the experience.*

Unlike Carole and Stevie, Lisa didn't own a horse. Her parents had offered a few times to buy her one, but she had declined, preferring to wait until she had gained more experience as a rider and could better select a horse that complemented her personality and riding abilities. Not having a horse had never presented her with a problem—she rode Prancer, a Pine Hollow Thoroughbred, so often that the mare almost seemed like her own. At times during the past couple of weeks, Lisa had almost felt guilty for not wanting to take Prancer to the Macrae Valley Open. But Samson's natural talent over jumps made him an obvious choice for the event.

What made the discovery of Samson's talent so special was that The Saddle Club had watched him grow from birth, when he was a leggy, awkward colt, to a sweet-tempered, high-spirited, sleek black horse. And his ability and training had been their secret and their project, although they had eventually let Red and Mr. Grover, a local horse trainer, in on their plan.

Once Max found out about his training, he helped The Saddle Club with tips and advice such as exposing Samson to a lot of different jumps to prepare him for the open. But he had let the three girls continue to work with Samson as much as possible over the last few weeks. Samson had taken every obstacle with ease and enthusiasm. He was clearly born to jump, and he knew it.

Veronica, on the other hand, was born to brag. She hadn't let up on her boasting about the Macrae Valley Open and how she was going to win the junior jumping event.

"Did you say blue, dear?" Mrs. Atwood asked, breaking into Lisa's thoughts. "Blue or green for your jacket?"

They pulled up to the tack shop. Lisa anxiously checked her watch. The shop was only five minutes from the stable, but she was due at Pine Hollow in half an hour for her last lesson before the open. She really needed to hurry with trying things on . . .

* * *

"STARLIGHT'S BEEN IN a terrific mood lately. I really think he knows he's going to a show," Carole said, fitting a bridle over her horse's head. As if in agreement, the bay gelding nodded his head. Then he nuzzled her neck while she fastened his bridle.

"Well, if anyone can read a horse's mind, it's you," said Stevie. She tightened the girth of the saddle on Belle, her bay mare. She spoke only half jokingly. Besides being the most experienced rider of the three of them, Carole also knew more about horses and stable management and could talk about them day and night.

"Are you disappointed about not competing?" Carole asked delicately. She still couldn't get over the fact that Stevie had volunteered to be tack manager for the show. During the early days of their Macrae campaign, Stevie had even offered to scout out Samson's competition, heroically spending time with Veronica to study her strengths and weaknesses. The three girls had once seen a war movie in which the commanding officer had advised, "Know your enemy," so Stevie had grimly started angling for invitations to spend time at Veronica's house. Despite her good intentions, Stevie had eventually given up on hanging out with Veronica. It had just proved too painful for both of them.

"Nah." Stevie shrugged in answer to Carole's ques-

14

tion. "I really want Samson to make his big debut, just as much as you guys, and Lisa was the one who discovered his talent. And you're definitely the most experienced rider from Pine Hollow. If Veronica hadn't taken over the other two stalls in Max's trailer, well, then I really would've put up a fight to go to the Macrae with Belle. But as things turned out, we'll just wait for the next big show, won't we, girl?" She gave Belle an affectionate pat on the nose and the mare nickered in response. "And then we'll take the blue ribbon in dressage."

Carole nodded, agreeing with Stevie's last comment. Carole, and everybody else in the world, never ceased to be amazed that Stevie, the zaniest and most disorganized member of The Saddle Club, was a star performer in the demanding, technical, intricate sport of dressage. In fact, Stevie's high standards and organizational skills for dressage—and her nonstop energy—made Carole and Lisa believe she might actually make a good tack manager for the open, and a good tack manager was extremely important. Max referred to the job as the "glue that holds together a good horse show performance." The tack manager was required to keep track of all the equipment, help people tack up for their events, and help care for the horses. In addition, the tack manager had to be prepared for every emergency from a missing button to a broken stirrup leather.

Just then Veronica sauntered in, leading Danny. Lately Carole and Stevie had seen Veronica around Pine Hollow more than usual—and more than they cared to—because she had been putting in a lot of extra time getting ready for the Macrae. Although Max was one of the best riding instructors around, Veronica's father had hired a battery of professionals from all over the country to prepare her for the open. And today the girls had watched her work with Johannes Wendt, a former member of the German Equestrian Team who was now a well-known instructor.

"Hi, Veronica," Carole called. "Has Danny been cooled down enough? He still looks hot." Like most people at Pine Hollow, Carole disliked Veronica, but she was unable to let that dislike get in the way of her concern for horses. Danny looked tired and was still breathing hard from the lesson. His coat was shining dark with sweat.

Veronica paused. "Oh, does he? Maybe I'll get Red to rub him down and throw a blanket over him," she said carelessly. She always fobbed her chores off on Red, who, because of the extra money Veronica's parents paid to board and care for Danny, had no choice but to comply.

Veronica cast a scornful glance over Carole and Stevie with their horses; then a smug smile appeared on her face. "My, that Johnny is just the best instructor in the world!" she trilled. "He taught me things about

16

jumping today that no *amateur*"—she looked meaningfully at Stevie—"would ever understand!"

"I thought that *Johannes*," Stevie said pointedly, emphasizing the rider's correct name and its pronunciation, "was an expert in dressage. That means you're probably wasting his time. He'd be better off working with someone like me."

Veronica laughed lightly. Sometimes Stevie's wit was too quick for her, but today Veronica's snobby armor seemed impenetrable. *Money and the best riding instructors*, Carole thought cynically, *could do that for you.*

"Oh, Stevie," Veronica said with a false smile, "you're so full of talk, talk, talk. We all know why *you're* not entering the Macrae. You're just scared, and you know you wouldn't have a chance on that backyard horse of yours. She may have some slight talent in dressage—no thanks to you—but as for jumping, well . . . better stick to trotting over the cavalletti with your little mare."

Stevie flushed with anger. Insults from Veronica were easy to match when they were directed at her, but when Veronica started insulting Belle, Stevie's wonderful, sweet, perfect horse, it made her so mad, she couldn't think of anything to say. In fact, she didn't want to *say* anything. She itched to push Veronica's face into a hay bale.

Getting no response from Stevie other than an angry frown, Veronica turned to Carole. Graciously deferring to Carole's experience as a rider, she said, "You and I can handle the big leagues, right? Obviously, we're Pine Hollow's only chances at the open."

Veronica knew that Lisa had entered the Macrae, so her comment got Stevie even more steamed. The implication was all too clear: She was completely dismissing Lisa. Well, Veronica didn't know about The Saddle Club's secret weapon, but she'd find out soon enough. Stevie smirked. *In fact, she might even find out now.*

Stevie was getting ready to charge out of Belle's stall and give Veronica a piece of her mind, but she caught Carole's eye. Carole was flashing her an unmistakable "Keep cool!" look. When Veronica glanced away, Carole pretended to zip her lips shut.

Stevie understood the gesture immediately. If she got into an argument with Veronica now, she was in danger of giving away their secret—Samson's jumping ability. And anyway, Veronica never seemed to grasp that Lisa was not far behind the most experienced riders in Horse Wise and could keep up with the rest of The Saddle Club very well.

As difficult as it was to stay quiet, Stevie gritted her teeth and finished tacking up Belle. "Just you wait, Veronica diAngelo," she said under her breath. "You're in for a big surprise."

Carole finished tacking up Starlight and answered

Veronica's last comment. "Yeah," she said, "it would be great if Pine Hollow had its own jumping star." Catching Stevie's eye, Carole winked.

Veronica tossed Danny's reins in Carole's direction and said, "Can you hold him for a second? I must find Red and ask him to cool Danny down. Then I've got to get going. I'm already late for my manicure." She vanished out the door.

Stevie rolled her eyes. "A manicure? How much do you want to bet that Veronica gets a full beauty treatment the day before the Macrae?"

Carole laughed. "I bet she gets the full treatment the day *of* the Macrae," she said. "I bet she's hired a stylist to follow her around and make sure her makeup doesn't smear and her hair is perfect."

Max appeared in the stable door. He looked cross and glanced at his watch. "What's with all the chitchat in here?" he asked impatiently. "Isn't it about time for our riding lesson?"

"Sorry," Carole and Stevie said simultaneously. After securing Danny and giving him a few sympathetic pats, Carole led Starlight out of his stall and swung onto his back. Stevie followed on Belle. Both of them paused to touch the good-luck horseshoe before heading out to the ring. All the riders at Pine Hollow did this because legend had it that no one who had touched the horseshoe before a ride had ever been seriously hurt. And today's lesson, the last before the Macrae Valley Open, promised to be an especially tough one.

"Where's Lisa?" demanded Max. Max could be easygoing about a lot of things. Promptness, however, was not one of them—especially when it involved a lesson he was giving. The Saddle Club had noticed that lately Max had become even stricter about his rules. They knew why: He had put in a lot of extra hours with them over the past few weeks, helping Carole and Starlight and Lisa and Samson get ready for the Macrae. Stevie had been allowed to join as reward for all her hard work at the stable and her generous offer to be tack manager. The experience had been well worth it. With Max's undivided attention—or at least with his attention divided only three ways instead of many—the girls had learned a tremendous amount about riding and jumping.

Even better, Veronica hadn't participated in any of the extra lessons, since she was so busy with her "professional" tutors. This had enabled The Saddle Club to keep Samson a secret from almost everyone except Max, Mrs. Reg, and Red O'Malley. During the regular Horse Wise meetings, Lisa had ridden Prancer.

Stevie shot a worried glance at Carole. It wasn't like Lisa to be so late for a lesson—it was much more Stevie's style, in fact.

"Lisa stopped at the tack shop, I think," Carole said

smoothly. "She should be here any second now. We'll tack up Samson and have him ready to go by the time she arrives."

Max's frown grew deeper. "Well, I don't want to start without her," he said. "Come get me when she's ready. I'll be in my office." He turned and walked out.

Carole glanced at her watch. She and Stevie dismounted, tethered Starlight and Belle to the fence, and got to work on Samson.

LISA YANKED OFF the breeches, leaving the legs inside out, and reached for her old pair. She was hot, sweaty, and tired—and she hadn't even started her riding lesson yet. "Mom, this pair is great," she said impatiently. "Please, please don't make me try on another pair. I just don't have time."

The tan breeches—the fifteenth pair she had tried on at the shop—had fit her perfectly, but Lisa was past caring about the fit. She put on her clothes and exited the dressing room.

Holding an armful of clothes, Mrs. Atwood gave Lisa a coaxing smile. "We're not done yet, darling," she said. She turned back to the salesperson. "We'll take the breeches, that new shirt, the new hard hat, and—

Lisa, are you sure? You don't want the custom-made boots?"

Hearing this last remark, the salesperson smiled at Lisa with a hopeful look. He was a thin young man with slicked-back hair, wearing a formal gray suit and a maroon tie. When Lisa had first seen him, she thought he would have looked more at home in an office than he did in the tack shop. He had not left her or her mother's side for more than a second, hovering over them and offering lots of unhelpful advice.

The Saddle Club had often frequented this shop to drool over new tack and clothes, and the group knew and liked the shop's owner, Ivan Elwood, very much. Ivan wore casual shirts and breeches, and anyone could tell that he himself was a rider and loved horses. He often shared humorous or thrilling riding anecdotes with customers, punctuating his stories by happily pointing to photos on the wall of favorite horses from his past.

But today Ivan was nowhere to be seen, and this man in the suit had introduced himself as James Reeds, "Ivan's nephew." Ivan had been forced to go out of town that day on urgent business, and Mr. Reeds had somehow persuaded his uncle not to close the shop, offering to fill in for him and his other salesperson, who was off competing in a horse show. "I'm trying to learn about sales from the ground up," he explained eagerly to Mrs. Atwood and Lisa. "I'm hoping to start working for this big water-heating company this year."

Water heating? Tack? The two things were so unrelated that Lisa felt a wave of dread. Who was this man, and what was he thinking, selling riding clothes and tack?

But wait a second, Lisa told herself. She wasn't a novice at riding, after all. She knew what a rider should wear to a big show, right? She could do this by herself, because, certainly, her mother wasn't being much help. Her mother seemed to care about three things—price (the more expensive, the better), fit, and color—and had no clue what riders should or shouldn't wear to a show like the Macrae.

Lisa suddenly remembered her mother's last question. "No, Mom, I don't need custom boots," she said. "I really need to get to my riding lesson. Right now."

"But, honey, Mr. Reeds said that Ivan could have them ready in two days, just in time for the Macrae," pleaded her mother. "Think of how incredible you'll look wearing those beautifully fitted new boots!"

Despite her anxiety about the time, Lisa was tempted by the custom-made boots. Wasn't this part of her dream—a new level of competition with the Macrae and new riding clothes to go with it? Hadn't she always pictured herself at a big horse show like the Macrae, wearing crisp new clothes and gleaming boots? Unlike the rest of her wardrobe, Lisa tended to wear her riding

24

clothes until they were completely worn out. She had a secret reason for this: When she had first started riding, she had made the mistake of wearing a brand-new, overly fancy outfit to her first day at Pine Hollow. After some good-natured teasing from Stevie, who always liked to have fun with newcomers to the stable, Lisa had vowed to break her clothes in and earn her riding credentials the hard way—through lots of lessons and practice. She had noticed the same thing in the ballet classes that her mother insisted she still take. The best dancers in her class often wore the rattiest leotards and tights.

Her riding clothes definitely looked worn in, although Lisa was too careful to let her clothes be ruined. But were they right for the Macrae?

She desperately wished that Ivan Elwood were there to give her advice. Although Mr. Reeds was extremely attentive and polite, he had spent five minutes trying to persuade Mrs. Atwood to buy some breeches that Lisa knew were all wrong for the Macrae—a special pair of European dressage breeches, the kind worn by top-level international competitors on the dressage circuit. "I don't need them for a jumping competition," she had said, over and over again until Mr. Reeds had finally given up. Even worse, he had tried to sell them the "latest revolutionary new fly spray; we just got it in." Puzzled, Lisa had kept on refusing to buy the fly spray. She eventually realized that Mr. Reeds didn't even know the fly spray was meant for the horse, not the rider.

After wrestling with her doubts and urges for a few minutes, Lisa finally made up her mind. Things were getting out of control, and she needed to get to Pine Hollow—now. She could just imagine what Max would say if she was late for the last lesson before the Macrae, and she didn't blame him. Between Carole and Lisa, Max had definitely spent a lot more time getting Lisa ready for the Macrae. His comments to her during lessons had been more pointed, and he had obviously paid more attention to her because of Carole's much greater experience on the show circuit.

"No boots," she said firmly. "I'll just polish my old ones. They'll be comfortable and they'll look great." She started walking toward the exit.

"Wait, wait!" Mr. Reeds called out. He sounded desperate, so Lisa stopped. He started pulling riding jackets off the rack. "You haven't even tried on any jackets. Didn't you tell me you wanted a whole new outfit?"

"Yes. Yes, we do," said Mrs. Atwood. She beamed at Mr. Reeds reassuringly. "And you've been so helpful. Lisa's just a little nervous about her lesson, isn't that right, darling? Now," she added firmly, "come back here and try on some jackets."

"My tweed jacket is in fine shape," Lisa answered tersely.

"Oh, come on, honey, let me treat you," pleaded

Mrs. Atwood. She held up a jacket. "Just try a few on," she said.

Lisa was just about to sharply repeat her refusal when she looked at her mother's face. Mrs. Atwood's cheeks were flushed with excitement and her eyes were sparkling. Lisa realized that the clothes were just a part of her mother's current state of happiness. Mrs. Atwood couldn't get over the fact that her little girl was going to ride in the Macrae. It was obvious that she wanted everything—including Lisa's appearance—to be perfect.

Lisa couldn't remember ever seeing her mother this excited about a horse show before. Since she'd found out that Lisa was taking part in the event, Mrs. Atwood hadn't stopped talking about it. "Top society people from Philadelphia and Pittsburgh attend this show," she had told Lisa. "Not only that, but people buy new outfits for the show—hats, gloves, you name it! You won't see any blue jeans among the spectators, no indeed! I'm going to go and mingle with the crowd and just enjoy myself, cheering my little girl on. I'll have to start shopping for new clothes right away. I think a suit, don't you? A pale color, like pink perhaps? And my double strand of pearls? Goodness, what will I wear the second day?"

Lisa knew that her mother was more interested in the prestige of the Macrae than in the riding that took place there. Even though her mother had always been a loyal spectator at the horse shows in which Lisa had competed, she remained in a constant state of bewilderment about Lisa's total horse-craziness. The people attending the Macrae and the clothes they would be wearing mattered a great deal more to Mrs. Atwood than the quality of the horses and riders competing in the show. Mrs. Atwood understood clothes better than competition, too.

Nevertheless, Lisa felt a pang of remorse. After all, her mother was just trying to buy her new clothes for the show. If she wanted Lisa to look nice at the Macrae—even for the wrong reasons—why should Lisa refuse so ungraciously? She hated disappointing her mother, especially when she was trying so hard with Lisa's favorite activity, riding. Lisa looked at her watch again. Her lesson was due to begin in ten minutes. *Pine Hollow is only five minutes away*, she reminded herself. Then she sighed.

"Okay, I'll try on a few," she said. Mr. Reeds immediately brought over a pile of jackets.

Lisa began pulling on jackets over the old blue shirt she was wearing. She tried on a dark gray wool jacket, and then a really nice one in hunter green. She was about to choose the green one, but then Mrs. Atwood suddenly brought a third coat over. "How about this red one, honey?" she urged, holding it out.

The coat was beautiful—bright red, finely woven wool, with black velvet lapels. It was undoubtedly the

28

most impressive jacket Lisa had ever seen, but she felt embarrassed to even try it on. As she and any horseperson knew, red jackets were referred to as pink and were worn by riders who rode with hunt clubs and competed in foxhunting events. Even though most clubs no longer used real foxes in the hunts, hunt club members still adhered to the traditional uniform of the hunt, started in England: the "pink" jacket.

Before Lisa could explain any of this, Mrs. Atwood slipped the jacket over her shoulders. "Oh, it looks wonderful!" she gasped. "Honey, take off that awful blue shirt—you need a white shirt to really see how it looks." She quickly hustled Lisa back into the dressing room and started handing her other clothes—a pair of black breeches, a snow-white shirt, a white stock tie. Dazed and increasingly worried about the time, Lisa found herself wearing a whole new outfit, with the red jacket as the centerpiece of the ensemble. She looked at herself in the mirror.

Not bad, she had to admit. The red coat with its black lapels looked striking with the black breeches. She turned slowly and examined herself from the back. She looked . . . almost professional.

Mrs. Atwood stuck her head into the dressing room. "Oh, darling, you look simply gorgeous!" she said, her eyes shining. She pulled Lisa out of the dressing room and made her stand in front of the three-way mirror. "Look at yourself! Just look at yourself. You look like pictures I've seen in books. You simply must get this jacket. Think," she added dramatically, "how incredible this jacket would look with that horse you're riding. Black lapels, black breeches, black horse. Honey, it's just the right accent. Thank God you're not riding a *brown* horse."

Despite her anxiety about the jacket, Lisa grinned. Her mother worked in retail clothes, and her most recent hobby was interior decorating. She clearly thought that a riding outfit and a horse could be coordinated like a couch and curtains. But Lisa looked at herself again in the mirror and frowned. Was the red—or rather, pink—jacket too showy? She had never worn such a flashy outfit to a horse show. Would Carole, with all her experience, wear a pink jacket to the show?

Lisa tried hard to think back on all her riding lessons and Pony Club rallies, but she couldn't recall a single time when she had seen Carole, or any other rider at Pine Hollow, wear a pink jacket. So few riders had attended horse shows as big and prestigious as the Macrae, and Lisa herself had seen pink jackets worn only by riders on television.

Suddenly Lisa felt a spurt of annoyance. She was hot from trying on clothes, the dressing room was cramped, Max and the others were waiting, and besides, she really looked great in that jacket. Why was she always looking to Carole for riding and horse advice? *Do I always have to compare myself with Carole?* she asked herself irritably. *Don't I have a mind of my own? And besides, haven't I worked really hard at my riding? It's not like I don't deserve a great new riding outfit.*

Impulsively Lisa took off the whole outfit and handed it to her mother. "I'll take it," she said. Then she remembered something and blushed. "Thanks, Mom, for everything," she said haltingly. "I can't believe how much new stuff I'm getting."

Mrs. Atwood beamed. "Lisa, you won't regret it," she declared. "You deserve the best, honey, and this is it. I'm so proud of you for riding at the Macrae."

"Excellent choices, Ms. Atwood," purred Mr. Reeds. Lisa saw that he could barely contain his joy at making such a huge sale. Jacket, breeches, shirt, tie, hard hat— he must be imagining what his uncle would say when he got back.

Looking at her mother's radiant expression, Lisa started to feel less guilty about letting her buy all those expensive riding clothes. She was shocked when she heard the price of the jacket. But Mrs. Atwood's smile didn't dim one bit, and Lisa sighed in resignation. "Guilt is bad for the digestion," she had often heard Stevie joke—just before digging into one of her strange ice cream concoctions.

Lisa leaned against the counter and waited for Mr. Reeds to finish wrapping up the clothes. Then she happened to glimpse the store clock. Her riding lesson had started twenty minutes ago! Panicked, she grabbed her mother's arm. "Hurry, hurry!" she said. "I'm late for my lesson—it's the last one before the Macrae!"

"What's that, this 'Mack-Ray'?" Mr. Reeds asked cheerfully. Exasperatingly, he started making small talk as he began to wrap up their purchases. "Some kind of dance?"

"It's one of the most exclusive horse shows, and all sorts of society people—" Mrs. Atwood began. But Lisa cut her off, grabbing the new clothes and shoving them into a bag. Then she dashed out to the car to wait while her mother finished paying.

On the way to Pine Hollow, Lisa begged her mother to drive as fast as she safely could. As a result, the ride only took two minutes instead of five, but Mrs. Atwood managed to get in five minutes' worth of oohs and aahs about Lisa's new clothes and the Macrae.

As they pulled into the driveway, Carole and Stevie came running out of the barn. Lisa barely waited for the car to stop before opening the door. Sitting on the edge of her seat, she hastily pulled on her boots and grabbed her crop and hat. Then Carole and Stevie reached her and pointed her in the direction of the show ring. "We've tacked up Samson for you—hurry!" Carole said urgently.

"As soon as I saw your car pulling in, I told Max we could start," added Stevie.

Lisa gave them both a grateful look. After she said good-bye to her mother, the group started walking quickly to the show ring, where their mounts waited. On their way over, Stevie asked, "Did you get anything? A new hat? A new crop?"

"A whole new outfit," Lisa admitted sheepishly. Before she could elaborate, the group reached the ring. Max was waiting by the fence, a tense look on his face. "Nice of you to join us, Lisa," was his only comment when they arrived.

Lisa apologized to Max, who waved her toward Samson. "We really have to get started," he said. But even Max's tension couldn't dampen Lisa's enthusiasm. She had new riding clothes, the Macrae was only two days away, and best of all, she was going to ride Samson— the most talented horse she had ever competed with in a show. She greeted Samson happily and swung onto his back.

I feel ready for anything, she said to herself.

3

As THE LESSON got under way, Max's tension eased and his usual calm, professional demeanor took over. Despite the anticipation in the air—or maybe because of it—the three girls really began to enjoy themselves. A private lesson with Max was a rare luxury. Although he always paid attention to each rider and horse in their group lessons, in private lessons he was especially focused and attentive to the finer points of riding.

First The Saddle Club warmed up the horses, trotting them across and around the ring in different formations and using different gaits. Then they practiced dressage moves, which helped the horses warm up and focus their concentration. Max watched the warm-up with a critical eye but made few comments—the group had been practicing so much during the past few weeks

34

that Lisa and Carole were extra careful about their seats and hands. Only Stevie, who wasn't getting ready for competition, goofed off a little. Max didn't bother to reprimand her. He just gave her a look that she knew all too well. She subsided immediately and went through the rest of the warm-up exercises with a docile air of obedience.

This lesson was the last time that Lisa and Carole would school their horses over a jump course before the show. The next day they planned to ride the horses lightly and then spend the rest of the day packing the horse trailer and van. Max had told them that horses needed a rest after a long training period and before a big event—otherwise, they might treat the event as just another day of training. He had also told them that the advice applied to humans as well and urged them to have a relaxing, fun evening and an early bedtime. The girls had made plans to watch a video and eat dinner at Stevie's house once everything was finished at Pine Hollow.

After fifteen minutes of warming-up, Max motioned the girls toward the jump course, which Red had set up to conform with specifications for the Macrae. "Who wants to go first?" Max called out.

Lisa looked at Carole. "You first," she said. She wanted to watch Carole and Starlight jump the course. She knew that this was one of the best ways to benefit from another rider's experience.

Lisa had watched many jumping events on television and had attended a few shows. She knew that in this class of the junior jumping division, form didn't matter. What mattered was jumping clean—getting over the course without any knockdowns, refusals, or run-outs—and finishing the course within the time limit. If a horse and rider knocked down poles or refused fences, faults were deducted from their overall point totals. If a horse and rider finished the course after the time limit ran out, time faults were deducted. Time really mattered if two riders had to compete in a jump-off to decide a winner. In the jump-off, the fastest time with the fewest faults won.

Lisa leaned forward in her saddle and peered at Carole, who had started Starlight in a canter and was heading toward the first jump. Lisa wanted to observe the other pair's every move—how tightly Carole made the turns on the course, how she controlled the pace of Starlight's canter as he headed toward each jump.

As Carole approached the first jump, she had a calm, set expression on her face. Stevie and Lisa, watching her, thought she looked as cool as a cucumber. Only Carole herself knew, however, that at that moment she was bubbling over with excitement and happiness. The prospect of competing in the Macrae, the long hours of practice, even the hours of stable work they had put in to convince Max to take them—all of that was heaven to Carole. And now her hard work in training Starlight was paying off. He was responding beautifully to her commands. He swept over the first jump cleanly and headed for the next. Carole urged him on and leaned forward at just the right moment. She didn't lose her balance when they landed but smoothly shifted her center of gravity until the next jump. Starlight was in fine form—he was obviously enjoying himself, and he cleared each jump with ease.

As Carole finished a clean round, a wave of clapping broke out. Startled, Carole looked around, then grinned and waved. Mrs. Reg, Red O'Malley, and some of the other students at Pine Hollow had gathered by the fence to watch the schooling and were applauding Carole's round and her nearly flawless riding. "And the blue ribbon goes to Carole and Starlight!" called out May Grover, one of the younger members of Horse Wise and the daughter of Mr. Grover, who had taken part in Samson's early training.

Although Lisa applauded along with the rest, Carole's almost perfect performance made her a little nervous. Even if this was only a practice round, it was one of the last before the show, and Lisa didn't think it would look so great if she made a major mistake. Stevie seemed to sense her fear, because she turned and grinned understandingly at Lisa. "Big fan club," she said. "You'll have to take Carole's ego down a peg or two," she added humorously, rolling her eyes at the impossibility of Carole's having a huge ego. Carole, as they both knew, was incredibly modest about her riding ability. She exuded a quiet confidence when riding, but she almost never bragged about herself—although she was definitely guilty of bragging a little about Starlight because she loved him so much.

Carole and Starlight trotted over to Max for his comments. "On the third and sixth jump, you were a little rushed," he said. "Although you want to guide Starlight toward each jump and encourage him to speed up a little to gain momentum, you got him racing toward it. He can easily lose control that way and take the obstacle badly and at the wrong angle. Light but firm pressure with hands and knees will help during those moments. Otherwise"—he paused and smiled at Carole—"I'd say you and Starlight did great. You're both ready for the Macrae."

Carole thanked him. She looked very pleased, and Lisa and Stevie saw her reach down and rub Starlight's neck.

It was Lisa's turn. Her heartbeat had gotten so fast and so loud, she felt it drumming in her ears. Before gathering up the reins, she wiped her hands on her breeches—both palms were soaking wet. She took a deep breath. She wiped her hands again. She adjusted her hat. She scratched her nose. She took another deep breath.

Then she realized what she was doing and silently laughed at herself. *I can't be this nervous—we're not even* at the Macrae yet! she told herself. *This is just a practice. Get a grip. Concentrate, concentrate.* Feeling herself calm down, she took up the reins.

"All right, Lisa—let's go," Max called out.

Despite her resolve, Lisa looked at the course and felt her heart begin hammering even faster. She couldn't ride this course. The jumps were enormous. What was she thinking, asking to ride Samson in the Macrae? Samson deserved better than her. Samson deserved someone as experienced as Carole. No, Samson deserved a professional.

"Lisa? Is anything wrong?" she heard Stevie ask.

Suddenly Lisa sat up straighter in the saddle and took up the reins firmly. "I'm fine," she said so loudly that Stevie and Samson both gave a little start. She looked over at Max and nodded, and he nodded back, still waiting for her to begin. *Don't be silly*, Lisa told herself. *Max wouldn't let you ride in the Macrae Valley Open, representing Pine Hollow Stables and Horse Wise, if he thought you were going to completely fail.* That thought didn't sound quite right—she certainly wanted to do better than avoid a complete failure. *I mean*, she corrected herself, *Max must have confidence in you to let you ride in the Macrae. He must feel you have a chance.*

She looked straight ahead at Samson's ears, which were pricked up eagerly for her signal to start. Confidence, Lisa knew, was a huge part of jumping. Determinedly she shortened the reins and cantered Samson in a circle. They broke out of the circle and headed for the first fence.

Samson sensed Lisa's sudden determination and increased his speed as they approached the first fence. He rose to the fence and cleared it with feet to spare. Although it was bad form to clear the fence with a wide margin of space, since that wasted the horse's energy, Lisa couldn't help feeling heartened at Samson's boldness. With a horse like this, who could *not* do well?

Samson cleared every jump with no problems. Although Starlight was a good jumper and a great all-around horse, jumping separated Samson from every other horse at Pine Hollow. He made it seem effortless, taking the obstacles as easily as if he were simply trotting around the ring.

As Lisa and Samson finished a clean round, another explosion of applause broke out among the spectators. "That's some horse!" Lisa heard May Grover say to another rider.

Lisa waved at Max and the audience with a relieved grin. Despite the number of hours she and Samson had spent on jump courses recently, she was always happy when the course was behind them and Samson had put in yet another terrific effort. To her astonishment, Max was clapping along with the rest of the spectators and grinning. If Lisa hadn't known better, she would have sworn that the expression on Max's face was almost one of glee. He seemed unable to contain his excitement that Pine Hollow—his own stable—had produced such a stellar jumper. "Good job!" he called out, almost shouting the words. Then he seemed to realize that he had just made an uncharacteristic display of emotion for a riding performance. He turned a little red and quickly called for Stevie to jump the course.

Stevie started Belle over the obstacles, but from the start it was clear that her concentration wasn't as sharp as it would have been if she herself had been training for the Macrae. She laughed as she and Belle knocked down poles on the first two jumps. Stevie turned the mistakes into a performance. She shook her head ruefully and then clowned around a little, pretending that she was sleepy and had just gotten out of bed and Belle just *happened* to be jumping a course. She slumped in the saddle, yawned a few times, and faked rubbing her eyes.

Red motioned for Stevie to stop. Grinning widely—Stevie could be irresistibly funny—he lowered the fences, and Stevie finished the rest of the course in a lazy, relaxed style. Although Max shook his head with almost as much disapproval as he'd shown approval at Samson's performance, everyone noticed that he had a little smile tugging at the corners of his mouth. Goofing off on a regular basis could teach a horse bad habits, but Stevie's occasional antics undeniably provided comic relief, especially during the recent stresses, and didn't disrupt Belle's normal training and exercise. With

41

Stevie, it was usually all or nothing—she was either hypercompetitive or ultra lazy. Carole and Lisa had often witnessed her fretting over a dressage competition and vowing to beat the other entrants, but they had just as often seen her put on performances like this one.

Watching Stevie finish the course and take an elaborate bow from the saddle, Lisa couldn't help wishing for a moment that she could be like her friend and take a break now and again from trying so hard. Although Stevie sometimes got into fights with her brothers or got frustrated when she couldn't see her boyfriend, Phil, enough, she never dwelled on things the way Lisa did. All Lisa's life—at school or taking part in the many lessons that her mother had signed her up for—she had strived for perfection. She worried over her grades, which were usually straight As; she worried over her ballet classes; and she even worried about silly things like embroidery.

Today, however, Lisa couldn't think depressing thoughts for long. The exhilaration from her first practice round was just too wonderful. Riding Samson, who jumped so easily and gracefully, was like dancing with a great partner. She was ready to jump the course again, right then, with none of the butterflies or sweaty palms from the first round. Lisa was surprised, however, that Max hadn't given her more precise criticisms after her round. *But after all*, she told herself, *what could be wrong with Samson's jumping? And how could I do better than a clean round?*

Max let Carole and Lisa try the course two more times, with Stevie good-naturedly retiring from practice to watch. Both times, Starlight and Samson jumped clean again. Then Max called the jumping to a halt and beckoned Carole, Lisa, and Stevie over with a pleased smile. "We can't risk making the horses sore two days before the show," he said. "Good job today. Let's do some trotting, and then you can cool them down. Remember, no jumping tomorrow. Tomorrow we'll check over all the equipment, make sure that all the tack is clean, and pack up the van. I've asked other Horse Wise members to pitch in and help us out with the equipment check and cleaning, but I expect," he said, looking sternly at all three, "to see a certain three riders logging in major hours in the tack room today and tomorrow."

Under ordinary circumstances, The Saddle Club would have emitted at least a token groan about the prospect of cleaning tack for hours. Although they realized that the chore was necessary, tack required a lot of elbow grease and patience to keep it in good condition. With the Macrae only two days away, however, the three girls didn't even make a face. They cheerfully agreed with Max and started trotting the horses around the ring.

After cooling the horses down, Carole, Lisa, and

Stevie took them into the stable and gave each of them an extra-special grooming—Carole and Lisa because of the Macrae and Stevie because Belle loved the feeling of the currycomb. Whenever Stevie groomed her, the mare stood very still and at times even closed her eyes, nickering in pleasure. "Maybe I'm scratching an itch that she can't reach," said Stevie, shaking dust out of the currycomb and starting on Belle's hindquarters.

Using a metal mane comb, Lisa carefully pulled strands out of Samson's mane to make it more even. She then began smoothing the hairs with a water brush. "Well, it's not like horses can just reach up with their hooves and scratch their backs," she said.

"True, but they can always scratch their backs against a tree, right?" said Stevie. "Don't bears do that?"

"I only hope that if there comes a moment when Starlight scratches his back against a tree, I'm not on him!" said Carole, grinning.

Laughing and chattering, the group finished grooming the horses and then fed and watered them. "TD's?" Stevie suggested when they had finished. TD's was the ice cream parlor where The Saddle Club often went after a day at the stables.

"Aren't you forgetting something, Ms. Tack Manager?" asked Carole.

Stevie looked blank for a second, then snapped her

fingers. "Oh, right, cleaning the tack. Darn. The growling in my stomach completely erased my memory. We'll put in a couple of hours and then go, okay?"

"I have an apple in my locker to tide you over," offered Carole. Stevie's appetite never ceased to amaze her or Lisa, nor did the crazy concoctions she ordered from TD's. Stevie could eat enormous amounts of food, and if her parents would let her get away with it, she would eat things like cookies for breakfast, lunch, and dinner—and not gain a single ounce.

"Thanks," Stevie said. "That should be just enough until I order my sundae. I'm considering peanut butter ice cream with pineapple sauce and coconut." Carole and Lisa wrinkled their noses and groaned.

On their way to the tack room, The Saddle Club passed a group of younger riders, all of whom had watched the day's lesson. The Saddle Club was well liked by the younger riders at Pine Hollow, and Carole often got asked for advice about riding and horses. She was known not only as the most experienced rider, but also as the person most willing to dispense information.

Today, however, the younger riders didn't seem interested in Carole and instead focused their attention on Lisa. "Lisa, do you think I can ride Samson? Just once, please?" begged May Grover.

"How about me?" chimed in Jasmine James, May's good friend.

Momentarily confused by the attention, Lisa said, "Well, Samson really belongs to Max, so I guess you'll have to ask—"

"Do you think you can teach me more about jumping?" interrupted Dawn Mooreland, a beginning rider who had just joined Horse Wise.

"Yeah, how fast do you want to be going when you make the turns between the jumps?" asked May.

Lisa's cheeks flushed pink. She was embarrassed by all the attention, but she was undeniably flattered by it, too. As long as she had been at Pine Hollow, no one had ever sought her out for advice about riding like this. Lisa had joined Horse Wise with minimal riding experience, but with frequent riding lessons, a lot of practice, and, of course, help from her fellow Saddle Club members, she had progressed very quickly.

One of Max's most important rules at Pine Hollow was that before a horse show, riders had to write down their goals for the show. He tended to frown upon riders who insisted that they wanted "to win the blue ribbon," even though Stevie, who could be pretty competitive, was hard to discourage in that area.

Lisa had written down her goals for the Macrae as soon as she knew she and Samson were to compete, and she had wisely kept them modest. "Gain experience in competing in shows like the Macrae," she had written.

Now, surrounded by a bunch of younger riders

clamoring for her advice, Lisa began to feel even more optimistic about her chances in the Macrae. Maybe she had a better chance than she'd thought to win the junior jumping division. Maybe she wasn't so far behind Carole, after all. And maybe what she lacked in experience, Samson would more than make up for with his incredible jumping talent.

"Well," she began confidently, in a style completely unlike her usual one, "when I ride Samson toward the first jump, I usually hold the reins like this." She demonstrated her grip for the younger riders, who hung on every word.

Stevie looked at Carole, raised one eyebrow, and grinned. Was this the Lisa they knew?

4

AT SIX-THIRTY IN the morning, Pine Hollow was usually a peaceful place. Few riders ever made it to the stable at that hour, and Red and Max were often the only people awake for morning chores. This Friday morning at six-thirty, the scene at the stable was completely different—one of constant activity and a lot of running around, mostly by Stevie, who was trying to coordinate the final loading of equipment and horses. The Pine Hollow horse trailer, hitched to Max's van, was parked in the driveway. The girls had cleaned it and loaded it with hay the day before.

Carole and Lisa were in the stable, bandaging the horses' legs and throwing blankets over them to protect them for the long ride. Max was discussing some last-minute business with Red, who was taking over the Saturday lessons while Max was away. Stevie, holding a clipboard with a checklist attached to it, was scannng the items in the trailer and marking them off on her list.

Although The Saddle Club had packed most of the tack and equipment into the trailer the night before, Stevie still wanted to make one final check that all the essentials were there. What Veronica defined as necessary, however, took up an entire stall of her own. Stevie confirmed, with disgust, that Veronica had no fewer than four tack trunks—Carole and Lisa had only used one each—and she also knew that Veronica's trunks were probably loaded with extra saddles, bridles, and other tack that she wouldn't even use at the show. Stevie had also been expected to load two bulging suitcases into the van for Veronica—suitcases stuffed with her extra riding outfits. Stevie did these things because she didn't have time to argue. Besides, she knew Veronica was going to get her comeuppance soon. That was enough to make Stevie smile while she lugged and loaded.

In addition, Veronica had demanded that Stevie find room for the special feed that she had insisted Max buy for Danny. Max was an expert on horse care and feed, and in the two weeks before the Macrae, he had helped The Saddle Club determine the balance of grain and hay that would maximize Samson's and Starlight's energy for the show. But Max's expertise wasn't enough for Veronica. She had pushed him to order the most expensive feed from his supplier, even though he had advised her that it wasn't necessary, and she had insisted that several bags of it be carted along to the Macrae.

After inspecting the van one last time, Stevie went into the stable, where Carole and Lisa were waiting with the horses. "Have you checked over your personal gear bags?" she asked them sternly.

Carole and Lisa nodded soberly.

"Okay then," Stevie said briskly. "Let's do a last-minute check of your gear. I've already inventoried the tack and grain in the van. Hair nets?"

"Check," answered Carole and Lisa together.

"Boot polish?"

"Check."

"Boots?"

"Check."

"Hard hats?"

"Check."

"Jackets?"

"Check."

After five minutes, Stevie marked off the final item on her list with a flourish. "Well," she said cheerfully, "that's everything."

Carole and Lisa looked at each other, then at Stevie, in complete awe. "I think she's had a personality transplant," Lisa said to Carole. "I've never seen her this . . . this . . ."

"Together?" finished Stevie, grinning. "Let me tell you a little secret. I've always been this organized. I just keep my organizational skills hidden when you're around, that's all. If I were this organized all the time, you'd confuse me with yourself. We couldn't have that, now, could we?"

Laughing, the three girls led Samson, Starlight, and Danny outside and loaded them one by one onto the horse trailer. After closing the gate of the trailer, they climbed into the backseat of the Pine Hollow van and waited for Max to finish talking to Red. Stevie, unconcerned by the early hour, opened a bag of cookies and offered it around. After hearty refusals from Carole and Lisa, she began munching.

Lisa looked at her watch. "Where's Veronica?" she asked.

Stevie laughed. "Oh, didn't you know?" she said. "Veronica isn't riding with us. She's flying to Philadelphia and then taking a limo to the show. She's going to meet us there. Darn," she said, suddenly frowning. "I should have found out who her driver was and given him the wrong directions to the Macrae!"

The thought of Veronica lost in the backwoods of

Pennsylvania in her ultraluxurious limousine made the group dissolve in laughter. When they had recovered, Stevie said, "Actually, we don't need Veronica to get lost before the show. She's already lost the competition, thanks to you two and Starlight and Samson."

Max climbed into the driver's seat of the van. "All set?" he asked, turning to the three girls. They nodded, and Stevie gave him a thumbs-up sign. "You're sure you haven't forgotten anything?" he asked, concerned. "We don't want to have to borrow or buy anything once we get there."

"Like a horse?" Stevie asked brightly. Max chuckled, and after Stevie showed him her checklist, he gave her an approving smile and asked no more questions.

Lisa looked at her watch again and frowned. "I wonder where my mother is," she said. "She said she was coming to see us off, but I guess she decided to see me at the show."

Mrs. Reg opened the door and got into the front passenger seat. After Max had found out that Veronica wasn't going in the van, he had invited his mother to ride along with the group instead of taking a separate car. She turned around in her seat and smiled at Lisa. "I think there's someone who wants to say good-bye to you," she said.

Lisa looked out the window and saw her mother. She stuck her head out and waved good-bye. "Bye, Mom!" she called out. "See you at the Macrae!" Her mother, she knew, was planning to leave soon and meet them at the show.

Mrs. Atwood waved in return. "Good luck!" she called.

Lisa was touched by her mother's gesture—that is, until her mother said, "I know you'll win, honey, especially with that new outfit!" Then Lisa couldn't help it—she rolled her eyes at Carole and Stevie. They grimaced understandingly. Parents just didn't get it sometimes.

Max started the engine and pulled out of the driveway. They were off to the Macrae!

THE FIRST HOUR of the ride passed smoothly. In the front seat Max and Mrs. Reg talked business about Pine Hollow. In the backseat the three girls laughed and joked around. Not only had Stevie remembered to check all the tack and equipment in the van, she had also remembered to bring games for the long ride—a backgammon board with magnetic pieces, a deck of cards, and other things. In fact, she had packed so many games and snacks that the van's backseat was quite crowded. Mrs. Reg, upon seeing the clutter asked with a twinkle in her eyes, "Are you sure you didn't forget anything, Stevie? Like maybe a volleyball net, a Ping-Pong table, and the contents of your refrigerator at home?"

The three girls took turns playing games and listening to music; each of them had a Walkman. But mostly they talked about the Macrae—what the show would be like, whom they would get to see.

Lisa was trying to ignore the queasy feeling in her stomach. She wondered if it was caused by the doughnuts she had eaten for breakfast. Carole's father, Colonel Hanson—an early riser thanks to his military career—had volunteered to take the group over to Pine Hollow that morning. Although he had offered to treat them to a hearty breakfast, the three girls had wanted to get to the stable so badly that they had only stopped for doughnuts on the way. Stevie and Carole had eaten three doughnuts apiece and appeared to be suffering no ill effects. In fact, Stevie had already polished off the bag of cookies she had opened and was just starting on some potato chips. Carole was complaining that Stevie was getting crumbs all over the backgammon board, but Stevie serenely ignored her and continued to crunch away.

The sick feeling in her stomach felt worse than doughnuts, Lisa decided. She was starting to recognize the signs of a nervous stomachache. She always felt this way before a big event, like a dance performance or a piano recital or an important test: sort of hollow inside, with a cold feeling in the very bottom of her stomach.

After another hour passed and there was no improvement in her stomach, Lisa finally decided to share her feelings with Carole and Stevie. "I feel sick," she said suddenly.

Carole and Stevie, in the middle of an electronic game of Battleship, looked up. "Sick how?" Carole asked, immediately concerned. "Are you feeling feverish?"

"Aching bones?" added Stevie. "Stuffy nose?"

"No, just my stomach," Lisa said. "Sick the way I feel before a test or a ballet recital. Sick as if something bad is going to happen to me. Do you think it's just nerves?"

"Definitely," Carole said reassuringly. "Before my first big horse show, I felt exactly the same way."

"I threw up before my first big horse show—twice," Stevie added helpfully. Carole gave her a grossed-out look but continued comforting Lisa.

"You just have to keep telling yourself that this is just a horse show," she said. "Even though it's one of the big ones, it's still just a horse show. You've done this before."

Lisa gave her a doubtful look. "The Macrae Valley Open is *just* a horse show?" she echoed. "I don't think so." She began to look even greener than before.

"Do you want some antacid tablets?" Stevie asked, picking up her clipboard. "I packed a first-aid kit." She rummaged around in a bag on the floor. As she offered the tablets to Lisa, who took one gratefully and popped it in her mouth, she intercepted an amazed look from Carole. "What?" she said.

"You really didn't leave anything out, did you?" Carole said. "I think all your hard work deserves a sundae at TD's when we get back—anything you want, our treat, and we promise not to make faces when you place your order."

"You've got a deal," said Stevie, shaking Carole's and Lisa's hands.

Max's voice interrupted their conversation. "Lisa, take a deep breath and look out the window," he said. "Horse show nerves are completely normal. Every rider, at one point or another, feels nervous."

"I remember this one rider," Mrs. Reg said dreamily, "a really talented rider, one of the best I've ever seen."

The three girls exchanged glances. Mrs. Reg was famous for her enigmatic stories—most of which had a lesson buried in them.

"So he was a great rider, and . . . ," Carole prompted.

"Even though he was a really terrific rider," continued Mrs. Reg, "with lots of talent and a promising horse, the prospect of his first national horse show almost paralyzed him with fright. Oh, he had competed a little bit around the local circuit—little country shows, nothing much. Always took the blue ribbon. But on the day of his first show, he wouldn't get out of bed."

"Did he oversleep? Did his alarm clock somehow

break?" Stevie asked sympathetically. Stevie's alarm clock sometimes mysteriously refused to go off, and as a result she frequently overslept. She always claimed that she had set the alarm the night before but it had somehow turned itself off before the morning.

"Well, he said he was sick," said Mrs. Reg. "But I knew better. He was scared. He was going from being a big fish in a little pond to a little fish in a big pond. And he was so frightened that he *did* look sick that morning—white as a ghost, shaking."

"Did he miss the show?" asked Lisa.

"No, no," said Mrs. Reg, smiling. "I managed to persuade him to go and talk to his horse before the show. I told him that his horse deserved an explanation as to why they weren't going. He thought I was crazy, but he went and did it—he was used to my crazy suggestions. And he changed his mind and went to the show."

Again, Carole, Lisa, and Stevie exchanged glances. Mrs. Reg's stories, besides being instructive, could also be obscure and difficult to understand. "I talk to Starlight all the time," said Carole at last, "but I don't think he's ever talked back—at least, not in words."

"Exactly," said Mrs. Reg. "When this young man went and talked to his horse, he had to explain to him that he was too frightened to ride in the horse show. And then he looked at his horse, who had just gone through weeks of training and grooming for the show and had done it all in grand style. His horse looked the picture of health—lively, alert, and ready to go! And he realized that all their hard work—both his work and his horse's—would be wasted if he let his fear get the better of him. So for the love of his horse, he went ahead and competed."

"How did he do?" Stevie asked anxiously. She, along with Carole and Lisa, had become completely absorbed in the story.

"He won the blue ribbon," Mrs. Reg said gently. "He rode better than he ever had before. And he went on to win lots of blue ribbons and cups. In fact, when he didn't have that sick feeling in his stomach, he sometimes did worse in a show than when he did have the feeling. Sometimes fear helps a rider reach new levels. As long as you don't let it keep you from doing something at all, fear can be turned into success."

The Saddle Club thought about the story for a few minutes. Max appeared to be concentrating on the road, and Mrs. Reg lapsed into silence. But out of the corner of her eye, Carole saw Max turn his head ever so slightly and wink at his mother. Light suddenly dawned. "Max, *you* were that rider in the story, weren't you?" Carole asked.

"Will you look at the time!" Max said, pretending not to hear her question. "We've polished off another hundred miles. We'll be there in no—"

The van jerked. From the back, the group could hear a distressed neigh from Samson. Max frowned, braked gently, and drove very slowly in the right lane. "I think we've got a flat," he said tersely. "I've got to take this exit—maybe we can find a gas station where I can change the tire with someone's help."

Once the van eased down the exit ramp, a gas station appeared right away. Heaving a sigh of relief, Max pulled into the station and parked the van and trailer. He turned to face the girls. "We've got to unload the horses," he said. "It'll be easier to jack up the van without a full load—and anyway, the motion of the jack would only make them nervous."

The three girls promptly got out of the van and went around to the back. First they unloaded Danny and then Starlight. At the gas pumps, other drivers who were filling up their cars smiled at the sight of the horses appearing from the back of the van. Three children popped their heads out of a nearby station wagon and started squealing and pointing at the horses. "Look, Mommy, horsies!" Carole heard one of them say. "Can we play with them? Can we go for a ride?"

Stevie hurried over to the station wagon. "Shhh," she said gently to the kids, putting a finger to her lips. "I know it's exciting to see horses, but these horses have been traveling for a long time and are getting tired and cranky. Don't you get that way sometimes when your parents take you for a long drive?" The three children nodded solemnly and quieted down. Then Stevie invited the kids to come over and pat

Starlight, who had the gentlest disposition of the three horses. The children were thrilled and gently stroked Starlight's neck. When Stevie returned the children to their parents, who were waiting by the car, the family thanked her and drove off.

Both Danny and Starlight were old pros at traveling and appeared undisturbed by the strange environment, the cars, the drivers, and the shrieking children. Samson, however, snorted and pulled at the lead shank as he backed off the ramp. While the group waited for Max to change the tire, Samson fidgeted nervously and refused to be calmed down. After Max was finished, it took half an hour of gentle coaxing and a few treats to persuade Samson to step back into his stall. Then the girls reloaded Starlight and Danny and closed the trailer. Mrs. Reg distributed bottles of soda that she had bought at the gas station, which everyone drank thirstily after the nerve-racking work of unloading and reloading the horses.

"Samson is pretty jumpy from the long ride," Lisa said to Max worriedly, "and we still have a few hours to go. What does this mean for tomorrow? Will this affect his performance?"

Max drove out of the gas station and headed toward the highway. "The way that horse jumps, I don't think anything could affect his performance," he said confidently. "Samson's a natural jumper—his talent will shine through tomorrow. And besides," he added, "I remember this one time when I was going to a show . . ."

"Here we go," Stevie whispered to Carole and Lisa. Max, like his mother, was also fond of telling instructive tales.

"We didn't have these fancy setups like we do today," said Max. "Just an old pickup truck and a trailer."

"Didn't you have to travel by chariot?" Stevie teased him.

"Ahem," Max said, then continued pointedly, "We had an old truck and a trailer. So we were riding along, and suddenly the truck broke down when we were still twenty miles away from the horse show grounds. And there were no gas stations nearby, and the truck's engine was just completely shot. Couldn't be repaired. But I just had to get to the horse show. So I unloaded the horse I was riding in the show, Duke, and I rode him the rest of the way. Made it in time for our first event."

"Wow," said Lisa, impressed.

"And then we took a first . . . No, was it a second? . . . No, I'm sure it was the blue . . . in the pleasure horse class, beating out my rival, Whitney Sorensen, by a nose. And let me tell you, girls, the only reason I won is because of the hours and hours of preparation Duke and I put into the show. Practice and hard work—that's what counts. That's what makes you focus: hard work and concentration. How many times have I told riders that good riding is ninety-nine percent hard work and one percent talent? Why, I remember a time when . . ."

Stevie nudged Carole and Lisa. "Wake me when it's over," she whispered. But Carole and Lisa were already asleep.

A FEW HOURS later, the Pine Hollow van pulled up to the show grounds of the Macrae Valley Open.

The group had expected to arrive at the show at least two hours earlier, but the flat tire and unexpected traffic on the highway had made them late. Everyone was stiff and tired from riding in the van, and all the work of unloading the horses, the tack trunks, and the grain still lay ahead of them.

At the sight of the show grounds, however, the group perked up considerably. The scene was incredible: four show rings, gleaming fences, and a huge stabling area off to the side. Spectators were strolling around. Lisa noticed that her mother had been right about the attire at the Macrae. The men were wearing suits and white shirts, some with ties, and the women were wearing pastel suits and dresses, some with hats and gloves. White tents with gaily striped canopies were set up around the perimeter of the area. Some tents sold food, Mrs. Reg explained, and others were used for viewing horses that were up for sale.

"Gosh, what a crowd!" exclaimed Stevie, rubbing her eyes. "We must really be late—it looks as if things have been going on for hours!"

"The show has been going on all week," said Max. "But the main events—the junior jumping division, a Grand Prix event, the hunt course final—are scheduled for this weekend. We could have come earlier in the week to watch, but I didn't want to spend that much time away from the stable, and I thought you could use the extra practice time."

Consulting the registration materials he had received before the show, Max found the Pine Hollow stalls on the map and drove over to unload the horses. After he parked the van, Stevie unloaded Danny, and then Carole quickly and smoothly unloaded Starlight.

When Samson's turn came, he refused at first to back down the trailer ramp. Finally, using her most soothing, cajoling voice, Lisa persuaded him to take a few paces down the ramp with the help of a carrot. And an apple. And three sugar lumps. As she eased him down, she saw three girls passing by out of the corner of her eye. They were wearing breeches, boots, and hard hats. Although her attention was occupied by Samson, she couldn't help noticing how beautifully put together the girls were. Their boots were gleaming, their shirts were snow white, and not a single hair was out of place. Lisa suddenly became aware of how rumpled she looked from the long ride, with her hair falling out of its ponytail and crumbs on her T-shirt from the sandwiches they had eaten on the way.

Halfway down the ramp, Samson jerked his head and snorted. Lisa managed to lead him down the rest of the way, but the minute his feet touched the ground, he began neighing loudly and tried to break away from her, dragging her a few paces and almost running over the three girls. Clearly, Samson was sick and tired of standing still in the trailer and wanted some exercise.

Carole and Stevie ran to help, and some other riders who were passing by immediately offered their assistance. Soon Samson calmed down. Meanwhile, the three well-groomed girls had moved off to the side and were making an ostentatious show of brushing off imaginary dirt, even though they hadn't been harmed in the least.

"What's this? The Wild West Show?" asked one of them scornfully. She had red hair and a turned-up nose and wore the most expensive-looking outfit of the group. As if she had said something wildly funny, her two companions laughed loudly at her remark. Then the redheaded girl went on. "I mean, it's like: Get control of your horse before you bring it to a show!" she said disdainfully. Then she turned to leave, motioning to her two friends—who seemed to be attached to her by an invisible string—to follow.

Lisa felt a hot wave of embarrassment at the way Samson had acted, even though she knew deep down inside that he was just tired and completely unused to long trailer rides. She also felt angry at the three girls. Weren't horse people supposed to stick together? Unfortunately, the more experience she got competing in horse shows, the more she realized that some riders weren't nearly as nice as most of the people at Pine Hollow. The nature of competition seemed to make a lot of junior riders act as if they hated one another.

"It's like: Only idiots stand in front of a ramp when people are unloading!" Stevie said, throwing her remark at the backs of the three girls, who were continuing on their way. They gave no sign that they had heard, but Lisa thought she saw the redheaded girl give a little flounce. That made her feel a bit better.

There was too much work to do to allow three bratty girls to distract them, so The Saddle Club got down to work. They walked the horses, unwrapped their bandages, and gave them some water. Then Max appeared. "How about saddling the horses and taking a quick ride to work the kinks out?" he suggested. The group quickly agreed—Carole, Lisa, and Stevie all felt as if they had some kinks to work out, too.

"Just stick close to the grounds and walk the horses, nothing else," Max cautioned. "I want the horses to get used to all the activity here—the people, the other horses. Don't take them on the main pathways, but don't get too far from the grounds, either. Just circle the perimeter. But who's going to ride Danny?"

"I will, of course," Stevie answered immediately. "Carole's got Starlight, and Lisa's on Samson."

Max shot her a glance. Stevie had a sweet smile on her face and looked eager and willing to exercise Danny. From experience, Max knew that when Stevie smiled like that, trouble often followed.

"Just make sure you bring him back," he said warningly, shaking a finger at her.

Stevie looked hurt and shocked. "Why, Max," she said, "I would never, ever—not in a million years!—allow my feelings for Danny's owner to affect my treatment and handling of an innocent horse. Even for the sake of our friendly little competition here."

Max sighed. "Yeah, right," he said. "And I can just somehow see you 'accidentally' loading Danny into a van that's heading straight back to Virginia!"

At this last remark, Stevie's eyes lit up. "Now, why didn't *I* think of that?"

Max grimaced.

Before Stevie could think about it any more, Carole nudged her. "C'mon," she said, "we should try to get in some riding now. The show grounds will close down for the night in a few hours."

The girls tacked up the horses, mounted, and headed off. Carole, who had attended the Macrae as a specta-tor a few years before, showed Lisa and Stevie some of the things she remembered from her previous visit. "That's where the judges sit," she said, pointing with her crop. "And over there is where the food tents are."

"Let's get a hot dog," Stevie suggested immediately.

"You're probably more likely to get a bowl of pasta salad," said Carole, laughing. "Or a pesto chicken salad sandwich. This show is attended by people who are pretty picky about what they eat. But don't worry," she teased, seeing Stevie's disappointed frown, "gourmet food at horse shows is pretty tasty, too."

As they continued their ride, Lisa felt some of her anxieties about the show return. The crowd of people milling around seemed better dressed and less friendly than any horse show crowd she had ever seen. The horses all looked incredible, well muscled with glossy flanks and proud heads.

With pride of her own, Lisa noticed that Samson, now that he was released from the van, seemed to be taking the entire scene—the crowds, the strange horses, the new environment—in stride. He was a little skittish, but he was curiously surveying the scene, swinging his head from side to side.

If only I could be that calm, Lisa thought. She became quieter and quieter until Carole suddenly said with authority, "Lisa, you have one of the best horses here."

"Really?" Lisa asked, in almost a whisper.

Carole nodded. "I haven't seen any horses that look as impressive as Samson," she said. *Except my Starlight,* she thought with affection—but she didn't say that out loud. She could sense how intimidated Lisa felt.

"Hey, you two," Stevie said excitedly. She had been riding a little ahead of them on Danny. She reined him in and waited for the others to catch up. Then she pointed at a group of people walking together. "Aren't those the number one, two, and three riders from the USET?"

Carole and Lisa looked, and sure enough, the three top members of the United States Equestrian Team were not more than twenty feet away from them, walking toward the stables. The Saddle Club had watched these three on television, riding in national and international competitions, but they'd never been this close to such famous riders. For the three girls, it was almost like meeting movie stars.

"There they are, in real life," Carole said dreamily. "I don't care if I embarrass myself by asking—I have to get their autographs."

"Just think," said Stevie. "They were probably junior riders like us once, wishing that they could get autographs of famous riders they had watched on television. I'm sure they won't mind. I don't care, anyway," she added determinedly. "I want their autographs too badly. I'd do anything for them, wash their horses, wash their van . . ."

Lisa said nothing at first. Although she was excited by the sight of the three USET members, she also noticed that they were wearing red—that is, pink—jackets, just like the one her mother had bought for her two days before. Then she remembered that neither Carole nor Stevie had seen her purchase. "Nice jackets," she murmured, tentatively looking at Carole and Stevie. "Don't you think?"

Carole put on what Lisa and Stevie described as her lecturing face, the expression she wore when she was about to dispense some piece of knowledge about horses or riding. "They are gorgeous, yes, but do you know why they're wearing them?" she said. "Red jackets are usually described as pink. The only riders who wear them regularly are those with at least four or five seasons of experience in the hunt field. And, of course, members of USET who compete in hunt events or are members of an official hunt club will traditionally wear that color. You'll also see hunting pinks on the British Equestrian Team, because so many more riders over there learn how to ride the open hunt course. I'm sure the three of them competed in the open hunt event—where they ride a course with obstacles like a brush jump or a ditch. Look, you can see the special patches they wear on the jacket to show the country of their team."

"Okay, knock it off, Professor," said Stevie, laughing. "Everyone knows red jackets are called pink, and everyone also knows who gets to wear them." Carole stopped lecturing and smiled sheepishly. She knew she had a tendency to get carried away.

After hearing Carole's little speech, Lisa felt a sinking feeling. Now she really couldn't admit her purchase of the pink jacket to either Carole or Stevie. Still, neither of them had said that non-hunt riders were *forbidden* to wear pink jackets, right? It wasn't as if there were a rule against her wearing a pink jacket in the Macrae.

More than ever, she wished she hadn't bought the jacket. But it was too late now.

"Uh-oh," Stevie said a few minutes later. "Trouble coming, straight ahead." Riding toward them on their horses were the three girls who had been present when Samson had been unloaded from the van.

Carole, Lisa, and Stevie had the eerie feeling they were looking at a mirror image of themselves—at least, what they would have looked like had they been rich and spoiled. The other three girls appeared to be exactly the same age as they were, and they were riding horses that matched the colors of The Saddle Club's

71

mounts: one black, one bay, and one gray. "It was like meeting our evil twins," Stevie said later.

Quickly checking over the other girls' horses, Carole had to admit they were impressive. The redheaded girl rode the black horse. He was bigger than Samson and had a white star on his forehead and three white socks.

Because the earlier run-in with the group had been so unpleasant, Carole, Lisa, and Stevie pointedly ignored the three riders and continued to laugh and talk among themselves.

As The Saddle Club passed the other three girls, however, they overheard the redhead say something about ". . . those girls and their circus ponies." Lisa immediately knew they were referring to Samson and her difficulties in unloading him, and she blushed in shame.

Stevie, who noticed Lisa's embarrassment, charged to the rescue. She stopped Danny and called over to the three girls. "Do you have a problem?" she asked challengingly.

With a bored expression, the redheaded girl reined in her horse, which stopped and snorted impatiently, and said to her two friends, "We don't have a problem, do we, girls?" She turned and looked condescendingly at The Saddle Club. "I'm Margie," she said. "This is Belinda, and this is Melinda. This must be your first time at the Macrae, so I guess it's understandable why you haven't learned how to handle your horses at a big show like this. We'll just forget the whole thing, shall we?"

"Belinda and Melinda?" Stevie repeated in disbelief. "Do all the names of your evil sidekicks rhyme, or just these two? Or did you make them change their names just to suit you?"

Margie frowned. "Hmmm, I guess there's no way of guaranteeing that people like you will know how to behave at a show like the Macrae," she said coldly.

"People like us? What do you mean? Good riders? Nice manners?" Carole asked pleasantly.

Just then, Margie's horse pulled his head up and snorted. During the exchange, Margie had kept her horse on a very tight rein, so his head had been uncomfortably high. Suddenly she eased off on the reins, and the black horse pranced sideways, almost bumping into Lisa and Samson, who were closest. Samson, as any horse would, pinned his ears back and shook his head warningly. Lisa, however, managed to calm him down quickly before anything else happened.

"My, my!" Stevie drawled. "Now who's putting on the Wild West Show? It's like: Get control of your horse before you come to the show."

Margie gave Stevie an icy look as she shortened her reins again. Without saying another word, she motioned to Belinda and Melinda, and the three rode away.

"Just as if she had a leash around their necks," said

73

Stevie, noticing how devotedly the two girls followed Margie's lead.

"I think we should head back," said Carole. "We're all starving, and it's time to let the horses rest for the night. And besides," she added, "this area has gotten a little . . . crowded."

"I can't believe how awful those three girls are," said Lisa. "Will everyone be like that?"

"Not everyone, no," Carole said. "But I'd forgotten how mean some horse show people can be. I wish the sport didn't attract snobs, but competing in horse shows usually takes a lot of money and a good horse. That's why you sometimes see these rich kids with bad attitudes who like competing because of the prestige and because it's an expensive thing to do. But I think we've just met the few rotten apples in the bunch. Not everyone is so cutthroat, self-centered, spoiled—"

"Hey, isn't that Veronica?" Stevie asked, pointing.

Unlike The Saddle Club, who were disheveled after their long van ride and dressed in their old riding clothes, Veronica looked as fresh as if she had just woken up and showered. And no wonder. As the girls found out later, the plane ride to Philadelphia had taken less than an hour, and Veronica had then ridden in an air-conditioned limousine to the show grounds.

Now she rushed up to Danny, greeting him with an ostentatious show of affection. "You sweet thing!" she cried, throwing her arms around his neck and kissing his nose repeatedly. Danny, startled by the sudden flurry of activity in front of his nose, pulled his head back and backed off a few steps.

After getting him to stand still again, Stevie raised her eyebrow—a sure sign of sarcasm to come. "If you love him so much," she asked, "why aren't you exercising him instead of me? Why weren't you there when the van broke down today and we had to unload and reload Danny? As a matter of fact, are you sure this is your horse? I'm afraid I'll have to see some identification before I let you take him, miss."

Veronica glared at Stevie. "Just because my parents want me to be comfortable and rested," she began, "doesn't mean that I have to take your— Why, what's this?" she suddenly said, noticing Lisa and Samson.

During Stevie's round of insults with Veronica, Carole and Lisa had completely forgotten about The Saddle Club's secret—Samson. Now Veronica was staring at the black horse with amazement. Although Samson was the son of Cobalt, Veronica had never taken much interest in the young gelding's training or progress. But now she was disconcerted by the sight of Samson, and the girls knew why. Veronica had assumed she knew exactly who her competition at the Macrae was going to be, and she was now discovering that she was wrong.

"Why are you riding Samson?" Veronica asked Lisa. "Where's Prancer? Has Samson even jumped before? Is he any good?"

"Well, he's—" began Lisa.

"After all, Cobalt *was* his sire," continued Veronica, not letting her finish. "And Cobalt was an amazing jumper—as all of my horses have been. Does Samson jump like Cobalt?"

76

"Well, he's—" said Lisa.

"How much training have you given him?" Veronica asked.

"Well, we've given—" said Lisa.

"And who else has seen him jump?" Veronica said. "How high has he jumped? How—"

"We've taken him over a few jumps, here and there," Carole interrupted smoothly. "He's shown some beginning talent," and here she paused, struggling not to giggle. Remembering the way Samson had soared over all his jumps, it was hard not to brag about him to Veronica.

"Really, we don't know anything about him yet," Stevie said casually. "We're just hoping to get him used to the atmosphere of a horse show—you know, get him some experience and exposure," she added with a straight face. After all, they weren't exactly lying to Veronica. They *were* hoping that Samson would become accustomed to the big-show atmosphere.

"I may ride him in a few classes, but I haven't decided yet," Lisa finished quietly. "Max wasn't sure if he was ready to be here, so we're just going to see what happens."

"Why are *you* riding him?" Veronica asked suspiciously. "I always thought it was a bad idea to pair a green horse and a green rider. Especially in a big event like this one. When you mess up, everyone who's anyone will know."

"Lisa's hardly a green rider," Stevie began angrily, but Veronica had already lost interest in the conversation. She tended to lose interest in any conversation that didn't concern her. Bored, she waved good-bye and walked off, once again forgetting about Danny and the obvious fact that he needed to be untacked, groomed, fed, and watered for the night.

The three girls made their way back to the Pine Hollow stalls. They were uncharacteristically quiet—Carole and Stevie because they were hungry and tired, and Lisa because she was smarting inside from Veronica's remarks about the green horse and green rider. Although Veronica had seemed fooled about the extent of Samson's talent, she had still taken the opportunity to ridicule Lisa for competing in a show like the Macrae.

True, Lisa had started riding and showing well after Carole, Stevie, *and* Veronica. But Carole and Stevie were always telling her how good she was. *And Max wouldn't have let me ride Samson in the Macrae Valley Open if he hadn't trusted me*, she told herself.

The more Lisa thought about it, the more focused her anger at Veronica became. As she untacked Samson and sponged him off, she vowed to beat Veronica in the jumping competition. *I'll show her*, she thought. *Won't she be surprised when Samson and I walk off with the blue ribbon?* she asked herself, forgetting, for the moment, that her goal at the show was to gain experience.

* * *

AFTER GIVING THE horses measures of grain and hay and making sure they had enough water for the night, the girls closed the stall doors and went in search of Max and Mrs. Reg. They found both of them leaning against the Pine Hollow van, talking merrily to an older man they all recognized—Jock Sawyer, a former USET member and an old friend of Max's and Mrs. Reg's. Jock had been a judge at a Pine Hollow schooling show in which The Saddle Club had taken part.

"Girls," said Mrs. Reg when she caught sight of them, "you remember Jock Sawyer, don't you? Jock, here are three representatives from Pine Hollow—Carole Hanson, who will be riding Starlight; Lisa Atwood, who will be riding Samson; and Stevie Lake. Stevie's one of our best riders, especially in dressage, but for this occasion she generously volunteered to be our tack manager. And I must say," Mrs. Reg added, smiling, "she's done a wonderful job so far."

"Good for you," Jock said approvingly, shaking Stevie's hand. "I learned a lot about horses that way, volunteering to be tack manager." Stevie glowed with pride at his approval and at Mrs. Reg's praise. They had all liked Jock—and he looked like their idea of a horse-person, with a tanned face and an easy smile and big hands. Even now, out of riding clothes, he still looked horsey. He was wearing a soft shirt and a worn tweedy jacket with leather patches on the elbows, and his legs were muscled and fit. He looked ready to jump on a horse at any second.

"Oh, and here's Veronica diAngelo, another young rider from Pine Hollow," said Mrs. Reg, catching sight of Veronica walking toward them. The Saddle Club almost groaned, but since Jock was present, they restrained themselves and waited politely for her to join them.

"Max! Mrs. Reg! Isn't this all just marvelous?" said Veronica, gesturing vaguely at the show grounds. She gave them a dazzlingly bright smile, which she then turned full force onto Jock Sawyer. "And who's this distinguished friend of yours? I *insist* on an introduction."

Mrs. Reg made the introductions with an expression of mild amusement. "You remember Jock," she said dryly. "He judged that event for us a while back."

"Oh, of course I remember you," said Veronica, wrinkling her forehead in concentration. "How nice you were to judge our little show! Especially," she added, glancing around, "since you obviously have much more important things to do."

Stevie, Lisa, and Carole all rolled their eyes at each other. The purpose behind Veronica's gushing was starting to become obvious.

"I enjoyed seeing Max's stable," Jock said quietly. "I always like to see young riders get caught up in the spirit of fair competition. Reminds me of how I began my own career."

"Yes, well," said Veronica, smiling. "You've certainly had a distinguished riding career. Now that you're not a member of the USET, I bet you're doing even more interesting things. Are you training horses? Teaching riding? Mmm, are you judging big events . . . like this one?"

Stevie telegraphed a knowing message with her eyes and eyebrows to Carole and Lisa, and they nodded in agreement. Veronica thought Jock was one of the judges for the Macrae! And as such she was buttering him up, hoping to win his good will. It was enough to make anyone sick to their stomach.

Jock, however, also seemed to grasp what Veronica was hinting at. He answered, with a twinkle in his eye, "Oh, I've been doing this and that. But no, I'm not judging the Macrae. I was asked, but I'm here on another mission."

Veronica's face fell. "Oh, you're not? Too bad. Well, Max and Mrs. Reg," she addressed them brightly, "I simply must get back to the hotel. Mummy rented a suite for us, and I'm sure she's going mad with worry over where I must be! We're going to eat in a four-star restaurant, you know."

"Sorry you won't be joining us for dinner, Veronica," said Mrs. Reg. "Maybe another time."

Veronica hastily departed, and The Saddle Club exploded in laughter. Max looked bewildered by the outburst, but Mrs. Reg and Jock grinned in understanding. "Guess I disappointed her by not being a judge," Jock said, shaking his head. "Things never change, do they? In my time on the junior jumping circuit, I remember meeting a few Veronicas here and there."

"Yes, we've already met our share," said Stevie, making a face.

"Not everyone's like that," Jock said. "Horse people are still my favorite people in the world. Can't get enough of the show circuit."

Out of curiosity, Carole asked, "What *is* your mission here. Are you just checking out the scene?"

"Well, yes and no," he answered. "I'm here as sort of an unofficial talent scout for the USET. I'm still in close touch with all the members, and they're really on the lookout for new talent."

Stevie promptly raised her hand. "That's me!" she said. "Where do I sign up?"

Jock laughed. "You know as well as I do that you have to work your way up through the show ranks," he said. "But it seems like you've got a pretty good start on that. No, I'm on the lookout for equine talent—for any promising horses that the USET can train for its team."

Max looked at his watch. "It's almost six o'clock!" he exclaimed. "We've got to rest up for tomorrow. But first, does anyone want to watch the elimination round of the Grand Prix event?"

Carole was the only one who mumbled tiredly in response, "Sure, Max." Lisa was resting against the van with her eyes closed, looking exhausted, and Stevie was clutching her stomach, miming extreme hunger.

Mrs. Reg laughed. "I think Stevie is trying to remind us that we're all starving. And I think Lisa is trying to tell us that we're all exhausted. Let's go and have dinner, and then check in at the motel. We all need some food and rest."

THE SADDLE CLUB gobbled burgers, french fries, and milk shakes at a nearby fast-food restaurant. Mrs. Reg insisted that the girls also eat a salad with their meal. "Got to have your vegetables," she said over the girls' protests that, surely, ketchup was a vegetable. Then the group checked into their motel, which had been chosen for its convenient location—only twenty minutes from the show grounds—and because it was a lot less expensive than the place where Veronica was staying.

Although Carole, Lisa, and Stevie had each traveled before with their families and with each other on a few occasions, it always felt special to stay in a motel together for a horse show. Since Mrs. Reg was in a separate room, they felt almost grown-up and independent, although they knew she would check on them if she heard any noise.

"I can't believe they don't have a pool here," said Stevie as Carole inserted their room key into the lock. "I packed my bathing suit and everything. I thought big motels like this always had pools. I wish we had picked somewhere else to stay. I wish— Hey, what's *that*?" As Carole opened the door, Stevie had glanced inside. She gave a whoop of happiness. Shouldering her way past her friends, she ran through the door and stopped in front of the large-screen television that dominated the room.

"Oh, did I mention that they have ninety-six channels here?" Carole said, grinning and dropping her bag on the bed. "The desk clerk happened to tell us that, but I guess you were too busy thinking about the pool."

"Pool? Who wants to go swimming?" Stevie said in rapture. She plunked down on the spare cot that they'd requested so that the three of them could share one room. "I'll take the cot," she said unnecessarily, since she was already stacking pillows, kicking off her shoes, and making herself comfortable. "After all, it's the closest to the television."

With a lot of not-so-gentle persuasion from Carole and Lisa, Stevie reluctantly agreed to brush her teeth and change into her pajamas. But after that she settled down on the cot, remote control in hand, and began seriously flipping channels. "Hey, look, I found a great film on the life of an Alaskan sled dog owner!" she called out.

"She's out of commission for the rest of the night," Carole said to Lisa with a chuckle. "I'm going to take a hot shower to relax, okay?"

Lisa nodded. "Sure," she said. "I promised to call my mother after we checked in."

Mrs. Atwood was staying at the same hotel as Veronica and her parents. She had tried to persuade Lisa to stay there, too, but Lisa had refused, knowing she would have much more fun sharing a room with Stevie and Carole. Digging a card with the hotel's name and number out of her bag, she plunked down on the bed and dialed. After a minute the hotel operator connected her to her mother's room.

"Hi, Mom, it's me," said Lisa when the phone was answered on the second ring.

"Lisa!" Mrs. Atwood said in a chirpy voice. "I was just looking over my outfit for tomorrow. Darling, I didn't see you at the show today. Did you get there okay?"

"Yeah," answered Lisa. "We had a lot to do, though."

"Did you see who was in the VIP box at the Macrae?" Mrs. Atwood continued in excitement. "The mayor of Philadelphia. Mrs. Grace Fairhill, the leading patron of the arts in Philadelphia. Mr. and Mrs. Charles Van—"

"Mom, I've just got to get some sleep," Lisa said firmly, interrupting her mother as she continued to list the occupants of the VIP box. Although she was glad her mother was having fun at the Macrae, she just wasn't interested right then in hearing about all the society people who were attending the show. She wanted to focus on her riding. After saying good night, Lisa hung up the phone and crawled into bed.

Carole emerged from the bathroom, wearing her pajamas and looking refreshed. "That felt great!" she said. "I could sleep for a week." She got into the other bed and turned out the light. Then she sat up again. "Stevie," she said firmly, "we've all got a big day ahead of us tomorrow. No more television."

"What did you say?" Stevie said absently. She was watching an infomercial advertising an exercise device that claimed to make muscles bulge.

Stretching out on her bed, Lisa joined the argument. "Television off." Stevie ignored her, too. Lisa sat up and looked at Carole, who nodded.

After a brief pillow fight in which Lisa and Carole stormed Stevie's cot and tickled her to get her to let go of the remote control, the television was turned off. Grumbling, Stevie turned out the last light and crawled under the covers.

The room fell silent for a few minutes. Then Carole spoke into the darkness. "I'm kind of having butterflies about tomorrow," she said softly. "I know Starlight will do well, but I'm the one who has to lead him over those fences. It's sort of terrifying, isn't it? All those people watching you. All those good riders we're competing against."

Hearing Carole's words, Lisa felt reassured. Carole had been to several major horse shows before, but maybe Mrs. Reg's story about the scared rider was true for all riders. Maybe nerves helped people do better than they normally would. "I have the jitters, too," she said comfortingly.

Oddly enough, though, she wasn't nervous at all. The sick feeling in her stomach seemed to have vanished completely. *It's all about having the right horse, one you're confident is a real winner*, thought Lisa. Maybe she wasn't the best rider, but privately, Lisa thought Samson might very well be the best horse.

"Don't worry about a thing," said Stevie in a confident tone.

"Why, do you know something we don't?" Carole asked.

"Yes," said Stevie in a near whisper. "I didn't want to tell you guys this, but I've been using the secret Horse-Master on Starlight and Samson."

"What's the HorseMaster?" asked Lisa, giggling.

"It's my new invention," said Stevie, imitating the obnoxious voice of the infomercial announcer. She turned on the lamp near her cot and stood on her bed, holding a hairbrush as a microphone. "It slices and dices vegetables, whips up your favorite shakes, and makes ice cream. It plays twenty-seven songs, and you can program them in random order. It's made of genuine plastic and Styrofoam, and best of all, my invention makes horses fly like birds. No jump is too big for horses who have used my HorseMaster!"

By now Carole and Lisa were starting to giggle. Stevie went on for another five minutes until a firm knock was heard at the door.

"Girls!" Mrs. Reg's voice called sternly. "Time to get to sleep. We have a big day ahead of us tomorrow." They heard her walk away.

Once again the three girls snuggled under their covers. Five minutes later, just before they dozed off, Lisa and Carole heard Stevie whisper something. "What did you say?" asked Lisa.

"I said," Stevie repeated, "seriously speaking, you'll do great tomorrow. After all, you've got the greatest tack manager in the world."

Lisa and Carole fell asleep, smiling.

LISA'S DREAMS THAT night were more like nightmares. On the first course she and Samson rode, she took all the jumps in reverse order. However, the judges felt sorry for Max for having such an embarrassing student, so they agreed to let her try again. On her second attempt, she had a clean round because she and Samson walked clean around every jump!

Morning, when it came, was a relief.

"Girls, are you up?" Mrs. Reg called, knocking on their door.

In the bed opposite Lisa's, Carole sat up and stretched. She grinned at Lisa happily. "Yup," she answered Mrs. Reg. "We'll be ready in half an hour." She looked over at Stevie, who was still curled up in a mound under the covers, with only the top of her head showing. Carole threw a pillow. "Hey, Tack Manager," she said. "Up and at 'em!"

The mound wriggled once, and then Stevie sprang up out of her cot. "I'm ready to go," she said briskly. "Who's got first shower?"

The group had agreed to wake up at six in the morning and be out the door by six-thirty. Lisa played Stevie in Rock, Paper, Scissors for first shower and won. Stevie began organizing their gear to take over to the show grounds. Carole washed her face, brushed her teeth, and braided her hair. The room suddenly seemed extra crowded with all the activity.

Lisa took a shower and scraped her hair into a hasty ponytail—she could always braid it before the event at the show grounds. She scrambled into her barn clothes and grabbed the garment bag holding her riding clothes. She had checked her clothes the night before to make sure they were still unwrinkled and fresh. When she had seen the pink jacket, she had cringed inwardly, remembering Carole's words about the USET members. But what could she do now? It was too late to get a new jacket—or even an old one.

While Stevie was dressing after her shower, Lisa went to the window and pulled the shade aside to check on the weather. Gorgeous sunbeams poured over her. The sky was a clear blue with puffy white clouds.

"What a beautiful day!" she said.

"No blaming any mistakes on the weather," said Carole, also taking a peek outside.

Because Carole had showered the night before, the girls were ready to go after Stevie had dressed and marked off items on her Saturday checklist. "Lisa, do you have your riding clothes?" she asked.

"Check," Lisa said breathlessly.

"Carole?"

"Check," answered Carole.

"Okay," said Stevie. "I checked over the tack last night before we left, so that's all set. I've got the sewing kit to baste your numbers on your backs, I've got extra hair spray and other beauty items just in case, and I've got the lint brush for your clothes. I think we're all set!"

The three girls joined Max and Mrs. Reg in the van. Mrs. Reg suggested they stop for a quick breakfast on the way. At first the three girls protested, saying they had to get to the stable and check on their mounts. "You need a good breakfast to start off your day," Mrs. Reg said serenely, "otherwise you'll look like a sack of potatoes sitting on top of your horses. We have plenty of time. Max has already been over to the show grounds to feed and water the horses."

When they got their food, Stevie grinned at Mrs. Reg. "Thanks for insisting that we eat," she said. "I can't believe I wanted to skip breakfast!" She dug into her French toast and bacon and ordered a chocolate milk shake to go, insisting that she needed the energy the sugar would provide.

Lisa could barely choke down one slice of toast. She was starting to get that queer, sick feeling in her stomach again, just like the day before. An unwanted memory came into her mind; she tried to push it away but couldn't help remembering anyway. Lisa had competed in a big horse show once before—Briarwood. She had asked Max if she could enter with Prancer, and Max had expressed reservations, saying that neither horse nor rider was ready for such a big show.

Because of Lisa's hard work and practice, she eventually won the argument. In a way, Lisa had been ready, but her horse hadn't been at all. Although she was a Thoroughbred with smooth gaits and a sweet disposition, Prancer also tended to be flighty and hadn't received enough training to overcome that in a big show. The pair had done poorly; in fact, Prancer had been disqualified, and Lisa had expected an "I told you so" from Max. But he had only patted her shoulder afterward and said that all riders and horses needed experience in horse shows, good and bad. Experience was what she wanted out of this one—but only good.

Lisa was quiet as they drove to the show. But when they pulled up to the grounds, she saw the morning sunshine illuminating the show rings and the flags and banners of the show waving in the breeze. Suddenly she felt a bit better. Yesterday all the flags, banners, and balloons had been for someone else. Today they were for her—and for Carole. Suddenly it wasn't just the Macrae. It was a place where they were going to compete and show what they had learned, for better or for worse.

When they arrived at their horses' stalls, Lisa was pleased to see that Samson was alert and frisky after a good night's rest. As the girls got busy grooming their mounts for their big day, Lisa remembered her weeks of training on Samson and how easily he had taken every jump.

She began to whistle confidently. This show, she felt sure, was going to be different from Briarwood. At Briarwood she had taken a horse that wasn't ready, but today she had the horse that was everyone's dream.

IN THE STABLING area, the three girls gave Samson and Starlight a special grooming and braided their manes and the dockles of their tails. They oiled the horses' hooves until they were shiny black. They gave the tack a last-minute polishing, although they had spent hours cleaning the equipment before loading it onto the van. As Stevie went off with Max to collect their numbers, Lisa checked over Samson—his bridle, the girth on the saddle—one more time. The junior jumping division was scheduled to begin at eleven o'clock that morning.

In the middle of Lisa's and Carole's preparations,

they heard someone calling their names. Turning, the two girls saw Mrs. Atwood hurrying toward them with a big smile on her face.

"Here you are!" she said when she reached them. "I've been looking everywhere for you!"

Where else would I be? Lisa asked in silent irritation. *Taking a nap? Doing my hair?* After all, her mother knew she was due to go on at eleven o'clock, and the stabling area was a natural place to look for riders making final preparations. But Mrs. Atwood knew so little about riding and horse shows that she had no idea what mattered and what didn't.

As her mother gave her a big hello hug, however, Lisa's irritation vanished. Wasn't she about to ride a dream horse in one of the biggest horse shows of the year? Her mother couldn't help it if she wasn't interested in horses. Lisa knew lots of nice people who weren't interested in horses and riding, and her mother was the nicest of them all. And besides, she was lucky that her mother was there to give her encouragement and clap for her.

She smiled at her mother. "You look like you've been having fun, Mom."

"Oh, it's been heaven!" said Mrs. Atwood. "I could go on and on about the people I've seen and met. The people here are so much more sophisticated than our little Willow Creek crowd. But look, honey, you're not even dressed in your riding outfit. Let's go off into the van and I'll help you put on your beautiful new red coat."

Carole was checking the saddle on Starlight, but at Mrs. Atwood's last words she looked up, startled, and watched Lisa and her mother disappear into the Pine Hollow van. Had she heard correctly? Obviously Mrs. Atwood had meant "pink coat." *But surely Lisa knows better than to wear a pink coat*, she thought. *No experienced junior rider would wear a pink coat to a horse show.*

Then she gaped as Lisa emerged, wearing the red coat. Lisa had a slightly sheepish smile on her face. "What do you think, Carole? It's part of my brand-new riding outfit."

"It's—It's—" stammered Carole. She looked at Lisa helplessly; then she looked at the coat. She wondered if she should mention the mistake and wondered why Lisa had agreed to buy a pink jacket. Then she noticed Mrs. Atwood's beaming, proud face, and she knew that Mrs. Atwood had persuaded Lisa to get the coat. "It's nice," she said finally with a weak smile. She just couldn't say anything in front of Lisa's mother.

Maybe I can get Lisa alone later and have a private talk with her, Carole thought. *But how would that help her now?* she then asked herself, frustrated. She knew that despite Lisa's confidence in competing on a horse like Samson, she was also sensitive about her riding ability and vulnerable to criticism. Why should Carole point out Lisa's mistake during such a major competition? Knowing Lisa, the high standards she set for herself, and how much she worried about things like school and the Macrae, it was sure to destroy her self-confidence. Lisa would be furious at herself for making such a silly mistake and wouldn't be able to concentrate on her riding. It wasn't as if it was a *rule*. It was a tradition. People might be surprised, but she wouldn't lose points or anything important.

Stevie returned with their numbers. "Here you go," she said cheerfully. "Carole, you're number eighty-five, and Lisa, you're—" She stopped and stared at Lisa's pink coat. "Hey," she began in a surprised voice, "do you realize you're— Ow!"

Carole had unobtrusively pinched Stevie on the arm to stop her from commenting on Lisa's jacket, and Stevie, ever quick to grasp a situation, finished, "Uh, do you realize that you're number forty-four? That's, like, my favorite number! I think that my favorite, uh, football player wears number forty-four."

"You watch football, Stevie?" Lisa asked distractedly. As the time for the jumping competition drew closer, she was starting to feel nervous again. She took the number from Stevie and began to baste it onto her jacket with needle and thread, but her hands were shaking too much. Finally Mrs. Atwood took the number from her and finished the job.

"No," Stevie said lamely. "But I've got favorite players."

As soon as she could, Carole pulled Stevie into a nearby stall. "I thought I should get you out of there before your lies got too weird," she said.

"Thanks," Stevie said gratefully. "I got the message to keep quiet about that pink jacket Lisa's wearing, but I couldn't think of anything to say."

Carole nodded. "I know," she said. "Lisa obviously didn't realize what a tradition she's breaking. There's no official rule, but I thought everyone knew only members of hunt clubs and USET members who compete in the hunting division wear pink jackets. I didn't have the heart to tell her, though. Someone must have convinced her to try on the jacket and Mrs. Atwood finished the job, also not knowing any better."

"We can't let her go out like that," Stevie said decisively. "We have to tell her the truth."

"No," said Carole, shaking her head. "I've thought about that, and what would it accomplish? This is Lisa's first big show since Briarwood, and we all know how bad she felt about asking Max to let her go, even though she didn't do that horribly there. Prancer just wasn't ready. But Lisa needs all the confidence she can get. She's a great rider with a terrific horse, and if we pointed out the jacket mistake to her now, she'd just die of embarrassment."

Stevie listened to Carole's argument, nodding slowly. "You're absolutely right," she said. "And anyway, what does it matter? In the junior jumping division, you can wear a baby blue jacket with pink spots on it and the judges can't fault you on it. It's the jumping that counts."

"Well, they might try to fault you on poor taste, but I don't think they'd succeed," said Carole, laughing. The two girls made a pact not to say anything to Lisa and hurried off to catch Max and warn him about the jacket.

IN THE WARM-UP ring, the competitors in the junior jumping division—including Margie, Belinda, and Melinda—circled their horses slowly through different maneuvers. Stevie and Max stood off to the side and called out commands to Lisa and Carole for gait changes and other moves.

Lisa, riding Samson, tried to concentrate on the serpentine across the ring, but she couldn't help glancing at the other riders, especially Margie, Belinda, and Melinda. She noticed Margie's horse prancing nervously. Was that the sign of an eager jumper? Then she looked at Melinda and saw how calm her horse looked. Was he just reserving his energy for the competition?

Lisa also noticed, when looking around, that a lot of riders were staring at *her*. In fact, one rider across the ring on a dapple gray horse almost lost a stirrup because she was looking so persistently at Lisa and Samson.

Lisa looked down at Samson. Maybe they were all staring at her because her horse looked so handsome. Samson was a big, coal black horse with a well-shaped head and long legs—and today his coat shone brilliantly from the morning's lengthy grooming. He stepped confidently and looked every inch a champion. Lisa couldn't believe she was riding such an impressive-looking mount. She knew looks didn't really matter—what counted was the horse's talent and disposition—but all the same, she couldn't help being proud of Samson's appearance. And she knew that unlike some horses, Samson could definitely live up to his looks with his talent.

Carole also noticed the looks that other riders were giving Lisa, and, wincing, she realized that Lisa's jacket was attracting a lot of attention. In fact, she could clearly make out a simper on Margie's face. But thankfully, no one was saying anything, and as Carole looked over at Lisa and Samson, she felt sure that Samson's talent would make everyone forget Lisa's pink jacket. Well, almost forget—it was pretty hard to miss.

Samson and Starlight went through the warm-up beautifully. Lisa and Carole each felt her confidence increase as her horse responded smoothly to her aids.

As they finished warming up, Veronica appeared

with Danny, a second person who seemed to be a hired groom for Danny, and a third person who was obviously her weekend coach for the Macrae. Veronica didn't seem to notice how late she was and appeared to be arguing with her coach about something. The Saddle Club and Max ignored her.

With Stevie at his side, Max signaled Lisa and Carole to come and gather near him. "Now, we've been over this before," he began. "Today, Saturday, is the first round—the qualifying round. Only twenty riders will make the second round tomorrow. With the number of competitors in this event, that means—"

"—that we'll have to jump two clean rounds today to make it to the second round tomorrow," finished Carole, figuring out the odds in her head. "With so many good competitors, we're bound to have two rounds today to come up with only twenty riders tomorrow. That means we'll have to jump clean the first time, and to make it to tomorrow, we'll probably have to jump clean the second time as well."

"That's right," said Max. "But remember what I've always told you girls. Competing is not just about winning. I entered you in this show not because I wanted you to win but because I think you have a lot to gain in experience from competing in a show like this. You've all worked hard and made a lot of progress in your riding. Whether you advance to the second round or not doesn't matter. What matters is that you perform to your own personal best standards. Are we clear on this?" Lisa and Carole nodded.

"Good," Max said. "Then I have another announcement. I just got the order of competition, and Carole, you're up first."

A look of apprehension passed over Carole's face. She, better than any other rider from Pine Hollow, knew how incredibly difficult it was to go first. Riders liked to watch other riders do the course first and measure how different horses were reacting to different fences. Not only that, but going first was bad luck. Carole squared her shoulders and looked determined.

"Someone's got to be first," she said.

Max smiled at her. "Then let's go walk the course and review the jumps," he said. "We don't have much time."

TWENTY MINUTES LATER, the announcer called out the start of the junior jumping division. Carole rode Starlight out to the ring, saluted the judges, and swung her horse into a rocking canter. They headed for the first fence.

Watching Carole, Lisa applauded in her mind. Carole and Starlight were jumping perfectly. Carole made the turns between the jumps tightly, but not so tightly as to cramp Starlight's angle of approach to the next jump. As they neared each jump, Carole smoothly and slightly increased Starlight's speed. Carole herself looked relaxed and confident and completely poised in her seat and hands.

Lisa watched Carole come up to the last fence. At every jump, she had wanted to close her eyes, almost unable to bear the tension of watching one of her best friends compete. And she knew that in a few minutes, she herself would be out there, taking that big rail fence, cantering toward that vertical . . .

Then she realized that Carole and Starlight were finished. They had jumped clean, and loud applause broke out and continued until the next rider appeared. Carole rode back to where Lisa and Samson were waiting and pulled up next to them. She was grinning from ear to ear.

"Congratulations!" said Lisa. She leaned over and gave Carole a squeeze on the arm.

Carole smiled even more, but all she said was, "Thanks. That felt *great*. Starlight went like a dream." Then, Carole-like, she immediately became all business and started explaining the course to Lisa. "You have to watch the in-and-out—it's bigger than anything we've ever done before, and it's tough. But Samson shouldn't have a problem with it. Then be careful on the last double oxer. The turn from the last jump is tighter than you think, and you need to build up speed to take that jump . . ."

Quickly and thoroughly, Carole briefed Lisa on the

course. Then they turned their attention to the other riders and horses. Several riders experienced knockdowns and refusals throughout the course. As Carole predicted, the in-and-out especially gave a lot of horses trouble. It was two fences set close together, so the horse had to jump quickly over the "in" fence, take one stride, and then jump over the "out." Riders had to time the approach perfectly, landing and then urging the horse to jump again.

Then Lisa heard her number. "Number forty-four is Lisa Atwood, riding Samson of . . . ," the voice droned.

Her heart pounding, Lisa gave Samson a nudge. In a haze she entered the ring and saluted the judges. She was only vaguely aware of the crowd and the hush that awaited her performance. She turned Samson to the course and tapped his belly. He began to canter toward the first fence.

Watching Lisa ride, Carole felt a thrill of excitement go through her. As much as she loved Starlight, she couldn't help feeling emotional as she watched Samson—the son of Cobalt—compete in his first big show. She watched a totally focused Lisa and Samson approach a large wall and clear it. Samson was jumping like a veteran, flowing over each obstacle with grace and power. Lisa was so lucky to be able to experience this, and she definitely deserved it, having been the one who discovered Samson's astounding talent in the first place.

As the black horse continued to jump each fence with extravagant ease, Lisa finally began to look relaxed and happy on his back. Then suddenly the crowd gasped. "Oh!" someone exclaimed, and Carole grimaced in dismay. Lisa had ridden Samson over the in of the in-and-out at an angle instead of facing straight ahead. Although Samson had successfully cleared the in fence, he was left facing the out fence at an awkward angle, with only one stride to make the out jump successfully.

"Oh!" the crowd gasped a second later as Samson gracefully twisted his body to face the out jump and cleared it with ease—almost from a standstill. It was the kind of thing only a champion could do. Carole's heart lifted once more, and she felt a surge of pride in Samson. What a horse he was!

Lisa and Samson finished the course with a clean round. Riding back, Lisa wore a worried frown. Carole and Stevie met them and gave Lisa hugs and Samson approving pats on the neck. "I nearly messed up the in-and-out," Lisa said ruefully.

"Yes, but you got out of it okay," said Carole. "You won't make the same mistake next time. Now that you've actually been through the course, you'll do that much better next time. And congratulations, you got a clean round!" She hugged Lisa again.

Max appeared and smiled at Carole and Lisa. "Great work, both of you. Samson and Starlight both jumped wonderfully well, and you two handled the course with just the right amount of control and speed. Lisa, I have a few things I want to go over with you. The in-and-out is a really tricky jump, and you have to make sure that you're . . ."

Lisa started listening to Max's remarks, but then the realization of what she had just been through hit her. She had just competed in the Macrae! She had jumped a clean round with Samson.

"Hey, that's some horse," she heard behind her. Turning, she saw one of the junior riders, a boy with curly dark hair, grinning admiringly at Lisa and Samson.

"Who's his sire? Who's his dam?" asked an older man with silver hair.

"That's really an amazing horse," a girl said, coming up to join the small crowd that was starting to cluster around Samson. "Most horses don't jump like that until they're at least ten years old, with a lot of show experience and training."

Lisa couldn't stop smiling. She felt as if she had bubbles of happiness and excitement inside her. She remembered feeling this way when she had taken part in a school musical and everyone had complimented her on her singing voice and her performance. For the next two weeks after that, Lisa had dreamed of being discovered by a talent scout and going to New York to sing and dance on Broadway.

Today she felt exactly the same way: *A star is born!* Cheeks pink with pleasure, Lisa began to answer the eager questions coming her way.

A DOZEN MORE riders competed. Carole, Lisa, and Stevie caught some of the rounds and were again surprised at the number of knockdowns, refusals, and run-outs. Mrs. Atwood and Mrs. Reg joined them in the stabling area after almost all the riders had competed. They had been watching from the spectator stands but had come to find the girls to share their impressions of the competition. Although the girls had been watching some of the rounds, they were so involved in the event itself that it was hard to be objective.

After Mrs. Reg discussed the individual riders—and Mrs. Atwood commented on their outfits—they told the girls the good news. "We've been keeping score," said Mrs. Atwood.

"Only ten clean rounds so far," said Mrs. Reg, smiling.

The Saddle Club could hardly believe it. "Only ten clean rounds!" echoed Carole. "That means Lisa and I are going to jump tomorrow."

"Right. There's no need for a jump-off round today with the scores we've been seeing," said Mrs. Reg.

Max joined the group. He, too, looked excited about

the Pine Hollow showings, but all he said was, "Veronica's up on Danny. I know you girls have had your differences with Veronica in the past, but in the spirit of rooting for our home team, we should go and watch them. Besides, you can always learn from watching someone else's riding."

"Yeah, I learned how to spend obscene amounts of money on my horse, on my riding clothes, and on countless riding instructors that I don't listen to," Stevie whispered to Carole, who giggled but dragged her to watch Veronica anyway.

Although Veronica was often a lazy, careless rider, she also had a lot of natural ability, loath as The Saddle Club was to admit it. When she chose to, she could ride well, especially when she was on a champion like Danny. Danny was a Thoroughbred who lived up to his show name, Go for Blue. While The Saddle Club often said he was just a push-button horse, he and Veronica made a good team. Today was no exception, and Danny cleared the fences easily. Another clean round had been chalked up for Pine Hollow.

"Okay, the Pine Hollow gang has permission to adjourn from serious riding for now and have some serious fun," said Max, delighted. He knew the girls would want to wander around the show grounds and look at the horses for sale and catch glimpses of famous riders. But Veronica, who had just joined them after competing in her round, shook her head.

"I can't go anywhere. I have to watch my friend, who's up next. She's the best rider here, next to me," she said loftily, staying put.

"Who's your friend?" Lisa asked politely.

"Just my best friend from riding camp," said Veronica.

The three girls knew that every summer Veronica attended a super-snobby, expensive riding camp where none of the campers had to do stable chores or even untack their mounts. Grooms took care of everything while the campers lounged around and took occasional rides and ate gourmet meals.

"When have you ever seen Veronica support anyone but herself?" asked Stevie in disbelief.

"Never," said Lisa.

"Let's check out who this friend is," said Carole.

The Saddle Club's growing suspicion about Veronica's friend was confirmed when they saw Margie ride out on her black horse and heard Veronica clap loudly when her name was announced. "Oh, it's just too awful of a coincidence that those two are friends," Stevie said, groaning and clutching her head. "It's like a mass of evil people that just keeps getting bigger and bigger."

"Birds of a feather," commented Carole.

"More like toads of a wart," grumbled Stevie.

Nevertheless, the three girls watched Margie and her black horse jump the course. Unlike good riders, whose aids to their mounts were often invisible, the group noticed that Maggie yanked cruelly on the reins to steer her horse in the right direction and kept reining him in too tightly after the jumps. Even so, the black horse jumped well. Like Danny, he was clearly a natural jumper. Even though his back hoof hit a rail and made it wobble, it stayed up, and Margie finished with a clean round.

Veronica made an extravagant show of support for her friend, clapping loudly. The Saddle Club swiveled their heads in astonishment at the sight of Veronica cheering someone else on. "I knew you could do it, Margie!" Veronica cried as Margie rode into the stabling area.

"Thanks, Veronica," Margie said graciously. "You rode well, too."

She dismounted and handed her reins to a waiting groom. "Bob, you can take my friend Veronica's horse, too," she said. "Let's go and eat some lunch. I'm dying for some chicken pesto salad, aren't you?"

Without glancing at The Saddle Club, the two girls walked off.

"Whew!" said Stevie, breathing a sigh of relief. "Does the air smell better around here, or what?"

"I have an idea," said Carole. "I think we should have a Saddle Club meeting over lunch. I'd like to discuss the course, figure out what we could have done better today, and plan a strategy for tomorrow."

Lisa, who was gazing distractedly at Samson, barely

heard Carole's suggestion. "What?" she said vaguely. "Oh, yeah . . . we should talk. Can you hold Samson for a minute? I have to go to the bathroom." She handed the reins to Stevie and went off in search of the bathroom.

LISA LOOKED AT herself in the bathroom mirror. She looked happy and glowing, just like someone who had a chance to win the junior jumping division at one of the most prestigious horse shows on the A circuit. Although she usually loved talking horses with Carole and Stevie, for some reason she felt reluctant today to have a Saddle Club meeting and discuss the course— again. Her elation at jumping a clean round at the Macrae was still too new, and she wanted to enjoy the feeling a little longer. *Do I really need to discuss the course with Carole and Stevie over lunch?* she thought. *After all, we both jumped clean rounds.*

However, Lisa had to admit that Carole, who was a relative veteran of these horse shows, was probably wise to want to discuss their performances. She smoothed some stray hairs and went into a stall to quickly use the toilet.

Just as she was about to leave the stall, she heard footsteps coming into the bathroom, then voices. Then she heard her name. Automatically, she froze and listened.

"I mean, that pink coat was just too much! I can't believe she bought and wore it! It's just so . . . so . . . *wrong*," she heard Margie's voice say.

"Everyone, even the most beginning of riders, knows that pink coats are only worn by real hunting people," said another voice that Lisa recognized as Belinda's.

Flushing hot with humiliation, Lisa looked down at her pink jacket. What she had secretly feared was true—she had picked the most inappropriate jacket possible to wear to a big show. Mortified, she whipped the coat off and began folding it into as tiny a bundle as possible. She wished she could just dig a hole in the ground and bury the jacket forever.

"Well, she is the greenest of riders," laughed another voice. With a sick feeling, Lisa recognized it as Veronica's. "She's hardly ever ridden before this. She takes group lessons at our dinky little stable, but she's got no talent and no experience."

"Even if she is a beginner," Margie said grimly, "she still somehow managed to have a clean round today. And that, my friends, just can't go on. Do you know what's at stake here? I've had a bit of slump, you know, over the past two years. If I don't win the junior jumping trophy here, my parents have threatened to take me off the A circuit! They said they can't justify the money they spent on my horse unless I spend more time training."

"Training?" a voice Lisa recognized as Melinda's said. "You don't need any training, Margie. You're perfect the way you are."

Normally Belinda's and Melinda's fawning over Margie would have disgusted Lisa. The remarks about her own pink jacket and her riding experience, however, had completely demoralized her. She waited, sick at heart, for the group to go away.

"Well, no novice is going to get in my way," said Margie in a harsh voice. "I've got a little idea, okay? Let's just drop a few choice remarks here and there, okay? Nothing too mean—we can't be too obvious. Just a couple of comments about her background and riding experience. And maybe just a *teeny* mention of that pink jacket."

"Oh, we won't have to work that hard to make her worry about things and mess up," said Veronica. "She doesn't really have any confidence. She only did well today because of her horse, which I might add was sired by *my* former horse, Cobalt. Anyone can ride clean on a horse like that."

Lisa's blood ran cold. Veronica's last comment was exactly what The Saddle Club had always said about Veronica and Danny. Was she now like Veronica? Was her success today due to Samson and Samson alone?

8

LISA FOUND CAROLE and Stevie still discussing the morning's competition. "Hey, Lisa," Carole said. "We were just talking about the other riders. You weren't the only one who had trouble with the in-and-out. Almost everyone misjudged that jump. And on the last jump . . ."

"Uh-huh," Lisa said mechanically. She took Samson's reins from Stevie and turned toward the stabling area.

"I thought that last jump was really tough," agreed Stevie. "But you guys both took it like a dream. Whatever you did today, do tomorrow."

"Did you see that one rider, the blond girl on the gray horse?" asked Carole. "She's pretty good. I've seen her at a few shows, and . . ."

As Carole and Stevie continued discussing the competition, Lisa made a few monosyllabic comments but otherwise stayed silent. The three girls took Samson and Starlight back to their stalls and began to untack them.

Finally noticing Lisa's nonparticipation in the conversation, Carole asked, "Lisa, are you all right?"

Lisa hesitated for a moment. Then she blurted out, "Why didn't you say anything about my coat? Why did you let me ride out in front of everyone dressed all wrong?"

"Oh, Lisa," said Carole, contrite. Immediately she guessed that Lisa must have overheard someone talking about the pink jacket. "I'm sorry, really I am. I did almost say something, but I only saw your jacket for the first time right before we were supposed to compete, and I didn't want to say anything that could damage your confidence. Besides, it doesn't even matter! Who cares what you wear? They don't score you on wardrobe."

"You could ride in pajamas, for all they care," said Stevie. "Well, not really . . . but you get my point."

Lisa thought for a minute. "I guess you're right," she said reluctantly. "I would have been destroyed if you had pointed it out to me before the competition. But I just overheard our evil twins and Veronica talking about me, and I don't know what I'm going to do about the jacket. I'm so embarrassed! I can't wear it again."

"Never fear, Stevie's here," Stevie said. "I brought my own blue coat, and you can wear it tomorrow. It may be a little large, but it's snug on me, so maybe not. But even if it is, at least it's not red—or scarlet—or whatever that thing is you have on."

"You brought your coat?" Carole asked, amazed. "Why?"

"Why, as a spare, of course," said Stevie. "You guys are just going to have to get used to the new, organized me," she added, grinning. "I'm finding your amazement at my preparation a little insulting. Was I really that bad?"

"No, never," Lisa said gratefully, "and now you're the perfect tack manager. I'd love to wear your blue coat tomorrow. Thanks so much, Stevie."

The three girls headed back to the show rings to see if any other events were going on. During their walk, at least seven complete strangers walked up to Lisa and began asking about Samson. Comments like "Where have you been hiding him?" and questions about his breeding and training at first had the effect of restoring Lisa's spirits. But after a barrage of questions about Samson and compliments about his ability, she began to get a little irritated.

"Why is it all about Samson, Samson, Samson?" she finally said in a peevish tone. "Why is it all about the horse and not the rider? Why hasn't anyone said one single thing about me? Is it because of the jacket?"

Carole exchanged glances with Stevie. Lisa still looked edgy after her encounter with Margie and the others, and they could tell that her confidence was starting to erode. "It has nothing to do with the jacket," Carole said. "It's just natural. All anyone looks at in the jumping events are the horses. They assume we're good because we wouldn't be here otherwise."

Lisa said nothing but continued to frown. She very badly wanted to ask Carole and Stevie a question about that awful conversation in the bathroom. But somehow she couldn't bring herself to raise the topic. She already felt terrible about the pink jacket, and now everyone she met seemed interested in Samson. She was afraid that if she asked the question, she might hear an answer that would make her feel even worse.

Replaying over and over again in Lisa's mind was Veronica's last remark, that anyone could jump a clean round with a horse like Samson. What Lisa wanted to know was, was it true? Was Samson the only reason why Lisa had advanced to the final? She knew that if she could bring herself to ask Carole and Stevie the question directly, they would tell her the truth, even if it meant hurting her feelings. But she didn't feel ready to hear the truth—if the truth happened to confirm her worst fears.

AFTER THE EVENTS of the morning were over, The Saddle Club returned to the Pine Hollow stalls. When they got there, they saw Jock Sawyer leaning against the van and talking with Max. Eager to catch any tidbits of horse advice and knowledge, the three girls moved closer and joined the conversation.

"He's some horse," they heard Jock say.

"Yes, we thought he would make a fine jumper—his sire was a champion—but we didn't know for sure until recently," Max said. "We trained Samson at Pine Hollow, and he spent a season with a local trainer, Scott Grover."

Max noticed that the girls had joined them. "Hi," he said, smiling. He turned back to Jock. "But if you really want to know about Samson's training as a jumper, you have to ask these three girls here. Not only did they help Samson enter this world, they also discovered his jumping ability and took on the bulk of his training over the past several weeks."

With a surge of hope, Lisa saw a chance to partly redeem her mistake with the pink jacket. "Well, I was the one who first discovered his jumping ability," she began. "I was exercising him and then I thought that maybe I could take him over a low jump. He cleared it like a pro! So then I brought Stevie and Carole into it. We realized right away that we had a natural jumper in Samson. We took turns schooling him over jumps. First we started low, and then we gradually took him over higher and higher fences."

"How high?" asked Jock.

"This high." Lisa demonstrated with her hand. "For a while, Samson was jumping too high over the fences, but we managed to correct him on that. We reined him in a bit more as he approached each fence and gave him leg signals to let him know not to overjump the fence."

"Interesting," said Jock.

As Lisa continued her recital, Carole and Stevie looked at each other, amused. Lisa sounded as professorial as Carole did when she talked about horses!

When Lisa finally wound down, Jock said cheerfully, "Well, that's just great. Uh, all your methods obviously worked in that you have such a terrific horse as a result. But thanks for sharing that information with me, uh . . . you're Stevie, right?"

"No, I'm Lisa," Lisa said, her face falling.

"Right, Lisa," said Jock, correcting himself and shaking her hand. "Well, I've got a lot of horses to check out this afternoon, so I'll be catching up with you later, Max." With a wave, he walked off.

Carole and Stevie didn't appear to notice that anything was wrong with Lisa or that she had fallen silent again after Jock had displayed such an overwhelming interest in Samson but called her by the wrong name. "I've had enough work for one day," said Stevie. "Let's go on an autograph hunt and take in the sights."

"I'm with you," said Carole, patting the pocket of her jacket. "I've got my notebook right here. Let me change out of my riding clothes and then I'll be ready to go."

"Not me," said Lisa. "I've got some things to do here."

"Oh, c'mon, Lisa," pleaded Stevie. "We don't get the chance to meet these riders very often. Let's have some fun."

"I'll introduce you to some people I know," Max offered. "Lisa, you really should take some time off today. Relaxation is as important as hard work in preparing for a big day. Besides, you and Samson did well today."

"No thanks," said Lisa firmly. "I'll find you guys later, okay?"

LEFT TO HER own devices in the stabling area, Lisa slowly changed out of her riding clothes—tucking the hated pink jacket into a deep corner of her bag—and into her barn clothes. She pulled down her tack, sat down on a hay bale, and began obsessively rubbing and cleaning the tack with saddle soap and polish.

She knew that she was facing one of her biggest challenges ever with tomorrow's round. She knew that Margie and her gang were, in general, not very nice people, she certainly knew what Veronica's character was like, and at any other time, she would have been able to brush off their comments. Today, however, was different. Although Lisa tried to focus on cleaning her tack, Margie's and Veronica's remarks kept replaying in her head, like a tape that refused to be turned off. She wasn't especially worried that their little plan would break down her confidence—now that she knew what they were up to, she'd be able to tune those comments out. But tomorrow's round looked like a whole different ball game.

When Lisa had first entered the Macrae, she had secretly fantasized about winning the event. But she hadn't really let herself believe that she could win, nor did she want that badly to win for her own sake. What she wanted was for the whole world to see what a wonderful jumper Samson was. After the conversation in the bathroom, though, the nature of the competition had changed. No matter how many times Max had tried to drill into her that winning wasn't important, Lisa wanted to win the junior jumping division and prove to people like Margie and Veronica that she was a lot better than they thought.

The only problem was, Lisa wasn't any more sure today that she could win the competition than she had been yesterday. In fact, she was starting to suspect that her clean round today was just a matter of luck and Samson's talent. If her confidence went down even further before tomorrow and hurt her concentration, could Samson alone save them? And if he did, what did that say about her?

Lisa put down the cloth she was using and laid her head on her knees. She felt exactly the same way she would if she were taking a huge test tomorrow, only this time she knew she hadn't studied enough. Lisa was such a perfectionist that she was rarely unprepared for a test in school. But in the rare instances when she hadn't studied enough, she had only managed to get her usual grade a few times. The other times, she had paid the price with failure—or, at least, with her definition of failure, which meant that she got a B-plus instead of an A.

With school, however, there was always another test and always another opportunity to get a final good grade in the class. Here, Lisa thought, there were no second chances. This was her chance to make it in the big leagues, the Macrae Valley Open. If she and Samson did well, she hoped Max would want her to continue riding the gelding in the big horse shows. But if all didn't go well, then Lisa would be once again—just like at Briarwood—a green rider, a rider who wasn't qualified to compete in the big shows.

Sitting on the hay bale, Lisa started to feel really sick to her stomach. Then she caught sight of something. Hanging across the aisle, outside Starlight's stall, were Carole's riding clothes, covered in plastic. Lisa gazed at Carole's old black coat, the ratcatcher shirt she'd worn to umpteen shows, and her old breeches. Everything looked neat, clean, and worn in. Compared to Carole's clothes, Lisa's outfit was stiff, flashy . . . and completely wrong.

Lisa's target of misery changed from herself to her mother, and she was angry. Why had she let her mother buy her a whole new outfit? Didn't she know better than to buy brand-new clothes for one event? And why hadn't she protested more when she had tried on the pink jacket? *I can't believe I actually thought clothes could make the rider,* thought Lisa. Her flash of anger made her feel momentarily better, since she was able to release some of her frustration. But deep down inside, she knew it wasn't all her mother's fault.

Maybe I should go hunt autographs with Carole and Stevie, thought Lisa. *And then maybe I should tell them how I feel. That'll cheer me up, I bet.*

Just as she got up, her mother appeared. Lisa sighed.

"THERE YOU ARE!" Mrs. Atwood said brightly. "Carole and Stevie said you'd be here. And they said to tell you that they've got tons of autographs, and Carole has asked some of the people to sign her book twice so that she can give some of them to you."

"Great," said Lisa. "I was just about to go and join them—"

"Wait a minute," said her mother. "I've got wonderful news. I met some very nice people today, and you'll never guess! They invited us out to dinner with them! We're going to one of the best French restaurants in town. The food costs the earth, but it's supposed to be wonderful."

Lisa was dismayed. Mrs. Reg had offered to take The Saddle Club out to dinner, since Max was dining with some old horse-show friends of his, and she would a thousand times rather do that than go to some fancy restaurant with her mother and her new society friends. She tried to think of a good excuse not to go. "Mom, you know I don't have a dress to wear to a restaurant like that," she said. "I just brought my riding and barn clothes with me."

Mrs. Atwood's smile vanished, and a slight edge crept into her tone. "Not to worry," she said evenly. "I went shopping in a local boutique and found you a darling new dress to wear tonight. No," she firmly cut off another protest from Lisa. "I just won't hear any more excuses. I've worked very hard to make friends here, and this is important to me. The least you can do is go to dinner. Is that so much to ask? Now let's go back to my hotel. I want you to try on the dress and get your hair done at the beauty parlor. We have a long afternoon ahead of us."

Lisa sighed in resignation. Looking at it from her mother's point of view, she seemed a real pain saying no to "dinner." She looked around and found a piece of paper, then wrote a note to Carole and Stevie explaining that she wouldn't be joining them for dinner and why. She also asked them to take care of Samson for the night. She tacked the note onto Starlight's stall where they would be sure to see it, then turned to her mother. "Lead the way," she said wearily.

* * *

124

LISA GAZED INTO the cold eyes of Margie, Belinda, and Melinda. Perhaps this was another dream, she told herself. Perhaps she was having a nightmare in which her mother's friends had turned out to be the parents of Margie, Belinda, and Melinda. Worse yet, she was forced to sit at one end of the table with them while their mothers chatted at the other end. *Perhaps I'll wake up*, Lisa thought, *and I'll be where I want to be—with Carole and Stevie and Mrs. Reg, eating at a pizza place and laughing and telling jokes.*

Then Mrs. Atwood, noticing Lisa's antisocial silence, suddenly reached over and tapped her daughter on the arm. Lisa jumped, but she didn't wake up. She was stuck with Margie, Belinda, and Melinda.

Then she looked down at the mess on her plate. She had asked for steak, cooked medium, hoping to get something that she recognized. Instead she had gotten a very rare piece of beef—oozing red juice—that had been wrapped in layers of overdone pastry. Lisa struggled with cutting the beef but could barely make a dent in the shell. When she finally managed to cut into the beef, the force of her knife made flakes of pastry and red meat juice fly over the front of the ridiculous new dress her mother had bought for her. The dress was pink and had smocking down the front, just like a baby's dress. *Thank goodness*, thought Lisa. *Maybe I've ruined it.*

"How long did you say you've been riding again?" Margie asked sweetly.

125

"Is this your first big show?" asked Belinda.

"Have you ever trained with any real riding instructors?" asked Melinda.

Lisa confined herself to answering their remarks as briefly as possible. Then they started asking her about Samson. Since this was more neutral territory, Lisa volunteered information more readily about him.

"Yes, I helped train Samson for this competition," she said proudly. "And I was the one who found out about his jumping talent."

"Well, of course you did," said Margie. "Who else but his owner would find that out?"

"Oh, I don't own Samson," said Lisa. "He belongs to Max. He's a Pine Hollow horse. I don't have my own horse."

"You don't own him?" asked Margie in disbelief. "How strange! I thought that everyone who rode the A circuit owned their own horse."

Lisa flushed. She turned away from the three girls and tried to get her mother's attention. But her mother was absorbed in a conversation with Margie's mother.

"Yes, it's the most exclusive store for riding clothes in the Philadelphia area, located on the Main Line," Margie's mother was saying. "You know, that's where anyone who's anyone lives in this area. We've all lived there for years. Although if you really want decent riding clothes, you should go down South to horse country."

"Really?" Mrs. Atwood said. "We've offered to buy a horse for Lisa, but she's turned us down so far. She says she's not ready, although after today, I can't see why not."

"Maybe that's for the best," said Margie's mother in a condescending tone. "After all, you can't imagine how much you have to spend for a halfway decent horse. Why, I spent at least . . ."

Hearing her mother's oohs and aahs, Lisa sighed. She was hoping they could skip dessert and the rest of this long, boring dinner so that she could get back to the motel. But it didn't look as if her mother was going anywhere for a long time.

"But you're from Willow Creek, right?" Margie's mother was saying. "I'm surprised you don't know Barb diAngelo. She's one of my best friends."

Lisa groaned inwardly. Of course Margie's mother and Mrs. diAngelo were good friends—just like Margie and Veronica.

"Oh, I do know Barb diAngelo!" said Mrs. Atwood. "We belong to the same country club."

"Well, you must join us in the VIP box tomorrow," Margie's mother said graciously, as if Mrs. Atwood had passed some important test. Lisa's mother beamed with pleasure.

Suddenly Lisa couldn't stand any more. She was sick of the food, she was sick of Margie and Belinda and Melinda, and she was sick of her mother's fawning over these awful people. "I don't think you need fancy riding clothes or an expensive horse to do well at a horse show," she burst out. "One of my best friends bought a horse for not very much money and trained him herself." Lisa was, of course, talking about Carole and Starlight. "She doesn't wear the latest riding clothes, either," she went on, "but she's one of the best riders I ever saw. She's competing in tomorrow's final jumping round."

During Lisa's outburst, Margie's mother began raising her eyebrows, and after Lisa was finished, she said, "Well, how . . . nice for your little friend, doing things that way. I'm sure she's very dedicated."

Mrs. Atwood, flushing pink at Lisa's outburst, jumped in quickly. "Lisa doesn't mean to be so . . . aggressive, do you, dear?" she said, patting Lisa on the arm. "The stress of competing must be affecting her manners. Normally she's just the quietest, sweetest little thing—such a good student, too . . ." She went on discussing Lisa as if she weren't there.

Excluded from the conversation, Lisa turned to her end of the table again, only to find Margie, Belinda, and Melinda wearing smug grins. Lisa's outburst had obviously convinced them that she was rattled and that their little plan to break down her confidence was working. "We'll see how you and your friend do tomorrow," said Margie with a meaningful smirk.

Fuming quietly, Lisa said nothing more.

128

"Would you like dessert, miss?" the waiter asked, handing her the menu.

WHILE LISA SUFFERED through *her* dinner, Carole, Stevie, and Mrs. Reg were eating their dinner at a nearby pizza joint. The restaurant, which smelled deliciously of tomatoes and cheese and garlic, was crowded with people from the Macrae. Carole and Stevie were craning their necks, stealing glances at all the famous riders. Their conversation consisted of phrases like "Look, there's . . . !" and "Hey, I didn't get her autograph! D'you think she'd mind if I—?"

"Yes, I do think she'd mind," interrupted Mrs. Reg. "Famous riders like to eat their dinners just as much as you do. And fortunately, our dinner has arrived."

The waitress placed a bubbling-hot pizza, laden with pepperoni and extra cheese, in front of them. The pizza looked so good that Carole and Stevie stopped stargazing and dug in as if they hadn't eaten for days. After polishing off three slices each, they resumed their conversation.

"That's the great thing about these big horse shows," said Carole, picking up another slice. "Nobodies like us get to rub elbows with Kathy Colefield!" Kathy Colefield, a show-jumping veteran, was eating pizza in a nearby booth. The girls had seen her win international competitions over the past year with her horse, Top of the List, or as everyone called him, Tops.

"No, no, you've got it backwards," said Stevie with her mouth full. At a glance from Mrs. Reg, she hastily chewed and swallowed and then finished her sentence. "At these big shows, Kathy Colefield gets to rub elbows with The Saddle Club!"

Carole and Mrs. Reg laughed. Then Mrs. Reg motioned to Kathy Colefield's booth. "Yoo-hoo," she called. "Kathy, don't you have time to say hi to an old friend?"

Kathy caught sight of Mrs. Reg and grinned. "Sure I do," she said, then excused herself to her fellow diners and came over to talk to them.

Carole and Stevie could barely contain their excitement. Carole had just read an interview with Kathy in a riding magazine the month before, and she knew that the rider was one of the leading contenders for a future Olympic team. Carole was almost too intimidated to ask her anything, but Kathy was so nice and down-to-earth, she put them at ease right away. She smiled at Carole and, thrilling her even more, said casually, "Nice job today. You handled that course really well, even though you had to go first."

"Th-Thanks," stammered Carole. Kathy Colefield had watched her compete? And now she was complimenting her?

"Watch out for tomorrow's course," said Kathy. "I've seen the junior jumping final lots of times, and I've noticed that they always like to use the same combina-

130

tion—a big oxer followed by a hundred-and-eighty-degree turn to a vertical. It's tough to get your horse around for the vertical, but I think you can do it." Carole glowed even more and thanked Kathy for the advice.

Then Kathy turned back to Mrs. Reg. "How's Max?" she asked. "I haven't seen him in ages. Is he here at the show? That rascal hasn't called me in years."

"These are two of his best students from Pine Hollow," said Mrs. Reg. "Of course he's here, but he had another engagement tonight. I'll tell him you said hello, though. He would love to see you sometime, I know."

"Wonderful!" said Kathy, her eyes lighting up. "Maybe I can come and visit Pine Hollow sometime, help out with a riding lesson? I'd love to get away from the show circuit. . . ."

Carole and Stevie looked at Mrs. Reg in excitement, pleading with their faces for her to say yes and encourage Kathy to visit Pine Hollow. But the expression on Mrs. Reg's face puzzled them. She was looking a little bit uncomfortable, a little bit understanding, and a little bit sympathetic. They waited for Mrs. Reg's response.

"Did you know," Mrs. Reg said gently, "that Max got married? He and his wife have a lovely daughter now."

Kathy's face fell slightly, but she smiled brightly. "No, but that's great news," she said. "Well, if I don't see him, give him my best." After wishing Carole luck, she walked off.

Mrs. Reg calmly picked up another piece of pizza, seemingly unaware that Carole and Stevie were practically bouncing out of their seats. "Okay, Mrs. Reg, give it up," Stevie finally commanded. "What was *that* all about?"

Mrs. Reg's eyes twinkled. "Oh, Kathy's an old girlfriend of Max's," she said lightly. "I guess she wasn't caught up on certain, er, recent events in his life. I know she took the breakup between them hard, but she was focused on her riding career and Max was determined to build Pine Hollow into what it is today."

Carole looked goggle-eyed in disbelief. "Max used to *date* Kathy Colefield?" Somehow she couldn't imagine Max with anyone but his wife, Deborah. In fact, she couldn't imagine Max dating at all.

Mrs. Reg smiled teasingly. "You know," she said, "back in the days when he was competing, Max was really quite a heartbreaker."

This last remark made Carole and Stevie giggle uncontrollably. The thought of their lovable but stern riding instructor as a dashing young man, breaking hearts on the show circuit, was too weird. Their giggles turned into laughter, and they were thankful that Kathy Colefield had already left, since they didn't want her to think they were laughing at her.

"Oh, oh," gasped Stevie, wiping her eyes. Her stomach hurt, she had laughed so hard. "I can't wait to tell Lisa that Max was once a major romantic idol on the A circuit."

"I wish she were here," Carole said wistfully. "I think this evening would have done her good. She seemed really tense after finding out about the jacket, and I could tell she was starting to worry about tomorrow."

"Me too," said Stevie. "Maybe," she added doubtfully, "she's having fun, too."

"Somehow, I doubt it," said Carole.

10

THE NEXT MORNING in the motel room, Lisa woke up suddenly before Mrs. Reg's knock on the door. She had been dreaming again—another nightmare. Once again, she was jumping the Macrae course. The obstacles looked the same, but this time the fences were about fifteen feet high. Although Samson was still clearing the fences with ease, Lisa was clinging desperately to his back, barely hanging on with her hands. In the background she could hear mocking laughter from the crowd. She looked for the source of the sound and saw Margie, pointing at her and laughing. When Lisa looked down at herself, she was wearing a clown suit, complete with floppy shoes.

When the dream finally ended and Lisa woke up, she was bathed in a cold sweat. Feeling tired and sick to her stomach, she quickly showered and then waited for Carole and Stevie to get ready. On the way over to the Macrae, the group again stopped for breakfast. Lisa refused to eat, saying, "My stomach just can't take it right now."

"Just a few bites of toast," Mrs. Reg insisted kindly. "It won't upset your stomach, and I really think you need the energy." Max, Carole, and Stevie all looked at Lisa, concerned. She was white and had dark circles under her eyes. But she told them she was fine. She didn't want them to worry about her performance today.

At the stabling area, things went from bad to worse. Samson ignored Lisa when she opened his stall, and he kept pacing restlessly. He shied away when she tried to cross-tie him and start his grooming, and he blew out his breath when she attempted to tighten his girth. "What's wrong with him?" she asked nervously. "Why won't he stand still? Maybe he can't compete today."

"He's fine," Carole said soothingly. "He just spent his second night in a strange stall, and we're the only things that are familiar to him here. He'll calm down." After yesterday's round, autograph hunting, a good pizza dinner, and a sound night's sleep, Carole looked refreshed and ready to go. But after last night's conversation before they all went to bed, she knew that Lisa was still feeling the effects of her awful dinner. She and

Stevie took Lisa aside after she'd finished tacking up Samson, and the group went into one of their huddles.

"Look, Lisa," began Stevie. "We can tell that you're still dwelling on last night's dinner, and we're here to tell you that you just can't do that. Remember how well you did yesterday. What a few jerks think is no concern of yours. Focus, focus, focus."

"You were one of the few riders who had a clean round yesterday," added Carole. "You'll do fine today, just as long as you don't let stupid things get to you. And besides, Stevie and I have a new Saddle Club project."

Lisa felt a spark of interest. "What's that?" she asked.

"If we even see Margie, Belinda, or Melinda come within ten feet of you," said Carole with a grin, "we'll bark at them until they run away. You won't be bothered by them again."

In spite of her friends' reassurances, Lisa worried that something was wrong with Samson. Had he eaten something he shouldn't have last night? No, that was impossible. Carole and Stevie had fed him, and they wouldn't have made a mistake. But maybe he hadn't gotten any rest. She examined him once again, looking over his flanks and feeling his legs carefully.

"Time to warm up," announced Max, poking his head over the stall door. Lisa's heart sank.

* * *

NOTHING WENT RIGHT for Lisa in the warm-up. Out of the corner of her eye, she could see Carole on Starlight, trotting across the ring. Then she started looking around to see if people were staring at her the way they had yesterday. She now knew that people had been looking at her pink coat, not at Samson. Even though she was wearing Stevie's navy coat today, she still felt self-conscious. Everyone must be looking at her and pointing and saying, "That's the girl who wore the pink coat yesterday!"

Lisa tried to concentrate on the warm-up. But it was as if she had forgotten how to ride. When she gave Samson the signal to canter, she started him too suddenly and he began on the wrong lead. Finally they started jumping over some low cavalletti laid out for the warm-up. Lisa rode Samson at the first one too quickly, causing him to take a huge leap over the two-foot fence.

Lisa almost lost her seat on the landing. Then she saw Max at the side of the ring, beckoning to her. When she and Samson pulled up, Max motioned for her to dismount and hand the reins to Stevie. He took her aside.

"Lisa, are you okay?" he asked in a low, serious voice. "You're not the same girl you were yesterday—did something happen between yesterday's round and today?"

"Oh, Max," said Lisa. "No one told me about the pink coat I was stupid enough to wear, and everything else has been going wrong since then. I just feel terrible."

"Is that what this is about?" Max teased. "A little fashion mistake? I thought we were going to focus on horses, not clothes." Then he looked at Lisa's stricken expression, and his tone got serious again. "Lisa," he said gently, "what color is Samson?"

"What?" Lisa said, confused.

"What color is Samson?" Max repeated patiently.

"He's black, of course," said Lisa.

"And what color is Starlight?" Max then asked.

Lisa was totally bewildered by now. "He's bay—you know that."

"Right," said Max. "And how did you finish the round yesterday? If I'm not mistaken, with a clean round. And how did Carole finish the round?"

"With a clean round," said Lisa. She was beginning to see where Max was going with this.

"Right." Max nodded. "So wouldn't you say that the color of the horse doesn't matter in the final result? I'm not saying that you were perfect yesterday, mind you. You have a lot to learn about competition—including how to handle your nerves before competing. Everyone's got them, but it's a matter of what you let the judges see and how it affects your handling of the horse. But I think you *can* learn how to be a better competitor, and I don't think it has anything to do with the color of your jacket."

"You're right," Lisa acknowledged reluctantly. But she couldn't make herself let go of Veronica's comment—that she was only there because of the horse she was riding. She looked Max squarely in the eye. "Do *you* think I can do it, Max?" she asked. "Do you think I'm ready to compete today?" Max's opinion of her riding ability mattered more to Lisa than anyone else's did. She really needed to hear his answer.

Max paused for a second. "Yes, I do," he said slowly. "I do think you can do it, Lisa, otherwise I never would have allowed you to enter a show like the Macrae. And your performance yesterday confirmed my belief. But at a time like this, it doesn't matter so much whether *I* believe you can do it. What matters is whether *you* believe you can do it. You're the one who has to go out there with Samson and jump that course, not me. I can't give you faith in yourself. Only you can do that."

Lisa absorbed Max's words of advice. Then she took a deep breath. "We can do it, Max," she said.

"I'm not going to let you go in there until I'm sure you're ready," Max said sternly.

"We can do it," Lisa repeated. She went back to Samson and mounted him while Stevie held him steady. Breathing deeply to calm herself down, Lisa summoned all her determination and tried to banish the destructive self-doubt from her mind. She rode Samson over a few more schooling fences and gave the thumbs-up sign to Max. He answered with a nod and a wave.

"Wow," said Carole, "this really is the Macrae Valley Open. Just look at that course."

The three girls were walking the new course with Max. It was formidably big and technical—eight obstacles in all, bigger than anything the girls had ever seen before. Just as Kathy Colefield had predicted, the combo of the oxer, the sharp turn, and then the vertical was there. The in-and-out was bigger than yesterday's version, and not a single fence looked like a giveaway. This was really a course to separate winners from losers.

The Saddle Club waited for Max to find out about the draw for the order of riders. When he finally got the list and informed them of the order, they were all astonished. Just as she had yesterday, Carole had to go first. Lisa, much to her dismay, was the last rider on the list. She didn't think she could stand waiting until her turn.

"I'm sorry, Carole," said Max. "It's tough, having to break in a new course again. The other riders will really benefit from your performance, but that doesn't help you much."

Carole shrugged and smiled. "Hey, that's horse

shows for you," she said cheerfully. Max patted her on the shoulder with approval.

A few minutes later, Carole heard her name, number, and Starlight's name being called. "Wish me luck," she said to the group, and rode off.

"What a pro!" Stevie said admiringly, watching Carole begin the course.

Lisa couldn't say anything. Her heart was in her throat as she watched Carole clear the first, then the second fence. Carole looked as calm as she had yesterday, and Starlight was responding beautifully.

But the course was much tougher than yesterday's, and although Carole anticipated the sharp 180-degree turn after the oxer, Starlight still hesitated as she rode him toward the vertical, and he jumped it awkwardly. One rail teetered and fell to the ground. As Carole finished the course, the crowd loudly applauded her performance.

As Carole rode Starlight back to where the group was waiting, she had a rueful grin on her face. "Not bad, but I didn't turn fast enough for the oxer-vertical combination," she commented as she dismounted. "I should have been preparing Starlight for the turn in the air!"

"No, you did fine," said Max. "Starlight was just spooked by how quickly the vertical came up after the turn, and you couldn't overcome it for him. A good job—I couldn't have asked for better."

Then Carole and Max began discussing the course with Lisa and Veronica, who had joined them after again being late for the warm-up. Veronica, however, refused to pay attention, and in the middle of Carole's discussion about the fourth fence, she abruptly excused herself. "I have to go and talk to Margie," she said. "Really, this is child's play for a horse like Danny, and I can get some advice from Margie's coach."

Max shook his head in disgust, and he and Carole kept on talking. Lisa was so nervous that she could barely concentrate on what they were saying, but she tried to look as if she were listening to their comments.

Then they heard Veronica's turn being announced. After a pause, they heard the announcer repeat Veronica's name and number in a questioning tone. "What the . . . ," said Max, going to look for Veronica. Obviously, she had gotten caught up in conversation with Margie and had almost missed her turn.

Hastily Veronica rode out to begin the course. She smiled prettily at the judges as if that excused her lateness, then made an elaborate show of affection for Danny. She started Danny over the fences, but she was so busy flipping her braid over her shoulder and smiling at the judges that she didn't pay enough attention to the course.

"Uh-oh," said Carole, watching. "I don't know if Veronica knows this, but she's completely left out one fence."

"No way!" Stevie said, gasping in amusement.

"Way," said Carole. "But I don't think she's realized it yet."

Still smiling and waving at her mythical adoring public, Veronica rode out of the ring. "How about that for a perfect round?" she asked, boasting to the Pine Hollow group.

"Uh, Veronica—" began Max, but he was interrupted by the announcer.

"Due to the failure to complete one of the jumps, Ms. Veronica diAngelo, riding Go for Blue, is hereby eliminated from the competition," intoned the speaker.

"What!" said Veronica. "They can't do that! I had no idea that I left out one of their silly fences. I'll have my father do something about this! Margie," she said to the redheaded girl, who had just pulled up next to them, "can you believe this?"

"Veronica, not now," Margie said impatiently. "I'm up next."

Just as she had yesterday, Margie went in and yanked her black horse over the fences. Despite her obvious lack of control, the horse jumped a clean round. Grinning triumphantly, Margie rode off the course.

As several other riders competed, Lisa got more and more nervous. The first round had eliminated so many riders that the competitors today seemed incredibly good. Everyone looked more experienced than she was. All the riders even seemed to be better dressed. Every perfect jump eroded Lisa's confidence another notch. The fact that all the other riders except for Margie had knocked down at least one fence didn't help Lisa one bit: She was convinced she would knock them all down.

After what seemed like forever, her turn came up. She dimly heard Max giving her some last-minute words of reassurance, but at that point, nothing could make her feel better. She didn't want him to worry, however, so she gave him a breezy smile and entered the ring.

All Carole's and Max's words of advice about the course completely vanished from Lisa's mind, leaving it blank. Suddenly everything around her vanished, too. She could no longer see or hear the crowd or her friends. All she could see was the first fence, and all she could hear was the wind rushing through her ears. She touched Samson with her heels, and he sped up eagerly. She felt as if their minds were joined at this moment, and that they each had the same goal: flight.

Watching nervously from the rail, the Pine Hollow group saw Samson and Lisa clear the first jump. Carole started biting her fingernails, and Stevie unthinkingly dug her own nails into Carole's arm.

When it was over, Lisa was stunned to find herself in the middle of an arena, surrounded by an applauding crowd. The PA system crackled to life. She heard the word *jump-off*. That was when, with a sickening jolt, she realized what had just happened. She had finished a clean round. Now there would be a jump-off between Margie and her.

The crowd erupted into new applause. Everyone loved the suspense of a sudden-death jump-off to determine a winner, and now they could sit back and enjoy the drama.

"OKAY, GANG," STEVIE said briskly, "we've got to prepare the champ. Lisa, do you need some water?" Lisa shook her head. "Okay, then. Carole, you take the lint brush and brush off Lisa's jacket. I'll walk Samson to keep him warmed up. Lisa, sit down and Carole will rub your shoulders in a few seconds to loosen you up."

The Pine Hollow group went into a huddle around Lisa and Samson to prepare while the course was reset for the jump-off. If both Margie and Lisa jumped clean, the one with the faster time would win the competition. Max explained to Lisa again how the scoring worked in the jump-off, then told her simply, "Keep your head up and go for it."

Carole nudged Lisa gently. "Look, someone's trying to get your attention," she said. Lisa looked and saw her mother in the VIP box, waving like mad. She was sitting next to Margie's mother, who didn't look happy at all when she realized Lisa was looking at them. As Mrs. Atwood continued to wave, Margie's mother glared at the Pine Hollow group.

"Whew, I'm glad I'm not sitting next to Margie's mom," Stevie said cheerfully. "Overprotective mothers are the worst."

As soon as it was set up, the three girls walked the jump-off course. It was short—only six fences. Three of them were raised higher than before. "How are you planning to jump it?" Lisa asked Carole nervously.

"I won't be jumping it," Carole reminded her. "This is just between you and Margie."

With a sick shock, Lisa realized that she wouldn't be able to watch Carole take the course and copy her movements. A stricken expression came over her face.

Max walked up to the three girls just then. "Lisa, you're starting to look as white as paper," he said. "Stevie, see if you can find her a light snack—some crackers to settle her stomach. Carole, let's go over the course with her. The more familiar you are with the course, the better off you'll be."

As Carole and Max started discussing the course, Lisa tried to pay attention, but the sick feeling just got worse. Suddenly she had the horrible suspicion that she didn't belong where she was about to go—into the ring for the final jump-off. *I've pulled a fast one on everyone,* she thought. *I'm here at the Macrae when I should have waited a few more years before competing in a show like this. Why did I try so hard to get into the show when I wasn't ready? I'm about to let down Carole, Stevie, my mother, and Max. I'm never going to be able to compete in a show of this caliber again.*

It was too late to fret about all this, Lisa realized. It was final exam time.

MAX GAVE LISA some final tips on the course. Then Stevie came up with a cup of water. Her face looked grave. "Lisa," she said. "They posted the order. You go first."

Lisa turned even paler and choked on her water. Max patted her on the back and, when she stopped coughing, said, "Don't worry, Lisa. Just remember what I told you: Don't rush. Even though you want your time to be faster than Margie's, the worst thing you can do is try to race through the course. That's where mistakes are made. Just keep your head up and go for it," and he gave her an encouraging smile. "You can do it." He paused. "Besides that, even if you lose, the worst it can be is second place at the Macrae Valley Open. Not bad, kid, not bad at all!"

Lisa gulped.

Several minutes later Lisa rode into the ring. Once again everything she knew about jumping vanished from her mind, leaving it completely blank. All she could think about was finishing the course and leaving it behind her. She pointed Samson toward the first fence.

As Samson jumped over the first fence, she could feel his confusion at the different fences. He was used to either jumping the same course again and again, as they had in training, or getting a day in between to adjust to a different course. He sensed that he was in the same place he had been just a half hour before, but the fences were new and strange. Lisa felt him falter slightly. At this point he really needed her encouragement and a firm hand and seat. She tried to pull herself together and directed him toward the second fence. Samson cleared it, and the third fence went by in a blur.

The tough oxer-vertical combination had been included in the jump-off course, except that the vertical had been raised by a few poles. "Turn in the air over the first fence," Lisa remembered, and she did just that, so that Samson was positioned correctly for the second jump.

Suddenly the blur around Lisa's vision receded and she saw the raised vertical clearly for the first time. It looked huge—bigger than anything she had ever seen before. *I'll never make it*, she thought in desperation, and a wave of panic engulfed her. Helplessly her hands dropped to Samson's neck, and the reins went slack. All she could do now was pray.

When the reins went loose, Samson hesitated, then sped up toward the vertical. Without guidance, he took off way too early and crashed through the fence. Lisa clung for one sickening moment to his neck, then fell against the fence as Samson trotted off with an empty saddle.

LISA SHOOK HER head. The two sets of crowds and fences in front of her slowly merged into one. She was aware of Samson near her left hand, head bowed in embarrassment, sniffing the jumping turf as if he might find a morsel of grass there. Lisa reached for the rein. Samson stepped toward her.

Across the ring, she could see a man in a white coverall running toward her. He carried a medical bag. He was coming to help. But Lisa didn't need help. All she needed was Samson. She held her hand up to stop the man and drew herself to her feet. There was scattered applause from the audience, but Lisa didn't know why. She was just doing what she was supposed to do. She was supposed to get back on the horse. That was what Max had always told her. She could do it.

Samson stepped closer to her. He knew what he was supposed to do, too. He waited patiently, never moving, while Lisa grabbed the saddle and hauled herself up onto his back again.

Again there was applause. The medic in the white coat stepped back to the fence, waiting, watching.

150

Nearby, Stevie and Carole were doing the same. In the VIP box, Mrs. Atwood watched as well, her hand over her mouth as if to stifle a gasp. All around, the world waited and watched.

Lisa touched Samson's side. He began walking. It felt natural, normal, like what was supposed to happen. At her signal he began to trot, circling the fallen poles from the fence they'd crashed. Then she signaled him to canter. Canter he did, right toward the next fence.

Oddly enough, Lisa's nervousness had vanished. Now that she had failed so miserably, there was nothing at stake. Lisa pointed Samson at the oxer, and he cleared it easily. Then she cantered the gelding down to the last fence, sailing over it. Everyone started loudly applauding and cheering. It was like one of her daydreams before the Macrae—only now she had ruined Samson's chances for the blue ribbon.

As SHE RODE out of the ring, she was surrounded by a crowd of people. Carole, Stevie, Mrs. Reg, and strangers pressed forward to shake her hand and congratulate her, but Lisa shrank back. She knew they were only trying to be nice after her humiliating defeat. She hastily dismounted and handed Samson's reins to Max. Then she looked around for an escape route.

Jock Sawyer came up and greeted Max. "Good job," he said heartily, patting Max on the back. "The girl got a little nervous, but it took a lot of guts to get back on the horse. And boy, can this horse jump!"

Although Jock's assessment was more than fair, it was the last straw for Lisa. As her eyes filled with tears, she forced her way past Carole and Stevie and the crowd and ran back to the stabling area.

Stevie and Carole looked at each other in dismay. Something was terribly wrong with Lisa—maybe she had been hurt in the fall. "Is it okay if we leave Samson with you, Max?" Stevie asked. "We've got to find Lisa and talk to her." Max nodded.

After several minutes of searching in the bathrooms and the stabling area, Carole and Stevie found Lisa weeping in the Pine Hollow van. Both of them climbed into the van and sat next to her. Stevie, who still hadn't recovered from her attack of organizational skills, found a clean handkerchief and handed it to Lisa.

After several minutes Carole said, "What is it, Lisa? Are you upset about the fall?"

"I cost Samson the blue! I cost Samson the blue!" Lisa sobbed. "If it weren't for me, he would have won the competition. He deserved a better rider."

"What are you talking about?" asked Stevie. "You did the best you could. Any rider can make mistakes. Carole knocked down a fence. Veronica left one out completely. Nobody expected any of us to take home a blue—and you're getting a red, amazingly good in a class like this."

"I don't care," Lisa said miserably. Suddenly it was as if a dam had burst open. Now that the competition was behind her and she'd failed Samson so horribly, she was finally able to talk to Carole and Stevie about all her doubts and fears of the past few days. "I started to think I wasn't up to riding Samson," she said. "The way people oohed and aahed over him, it became clear that I was riding in the Macrae because of Samson, not because of me. I'm too inexperienced. I'm too green, as Margie and Veronica rightly pointed out. I've been feeling sick to my stomach the past few days, knowing I don't belong here."

"Since when did you start listening to people like Margie and Veronica?" Stevie demanded indignantly.

But Carole hushed her and put an arm around Lisa. "Listen, Lisa, I don't know why you're beating yourself up about this," she said. "You may have made a few mistakes, but that doesn't mean you don't belong here. I argued for you to be the one to ride Samson because I know what a good rider you are, and Max agreed because *he* knows what a good rider you are."

"But I failed," Lisa said. "I embarrassed everyone."

"No, you didn't fail," said Carole. A note of sternness had crept into her voice; she was beginning to sound like Max. "You competed in a huge event—the

Macrae Valley Open—and you did well against really tough competition. You took a bad fall and you got right back up and finished the course in style. You've come farther in a short time than any rider I've ever seen before. Today you won. You might not have won the blue ribbon, but you won."

Lisa thought about that for a few minutes and stopped crying.

"And you took second place at the Macrae," said Stevie again.

"Not too shabby," said Carole, grinning.

"That wasn't me," said Lisa with a watery smile. "That was Samson."

"Funny," Carole said thoughtfully. "I could've sworn there was a rider on his back. You did a lot more than just go along for the ride, you know," she added. "Think about it."

A FEW MINUTES later The Saddle Club heard the announcer's voice. "Lisa, you've got to go and get your ribbon," ordered Stevie. Quickly she produced a cloth and held it under a nearby tap. Then she wiped the last traces of tears off Lisa's face. As a final flourish, Stevie took out a compact and applied powder to Lisa's nose, which had turned bright pink from crying.

"Stevie with a powder puff? Now I've seen everything," said Carole in disbelief.

"You look great," said Stevie, closing the compact with a snap. "Now go out there and get your ribbon!"

The three girls ran back to the ring, and Lisa mounted Samson. Carole got on Starlight for the awards ceremony, because as it turned out, she and Starlight had taken fourth place.

Together the two girls rode out to the judges' stand. As the red ribbon was pinned on Samson's bridle, Lisa felt a bit sheepish. Although she had cheered up a bit after Carole's talk, in her heart of hearts she knew that she had cost Samson the blue. She didn't even care that it was Margie who had won the blue ribbon—if it hadn't been for Lisa's mistake, Margie's horse wouldn't have stood a chance against Samson.

One of the judges leaned over to congratulate Lisa. "That took a lot of courage, getting back on course and finishing in style," he said. "That's the hallmark of a true winner." Lisa politely acknowledged his compliment, but it somehow didn't really register.

As the riders circled the ring to the applause of the crowd, Lisa started thinking over what Carole had said in the van. She wondered about Carole's last comment. What had Lisa done for Samson besides making him miss that fence?

As she felt Samson prance beneath her, the meaning of Carole's remark suddenly became clear. If Lisa hadn't discovered Samson's ability, and if she hadn't put in hours and hours of training with him, taking the time to exercise him and school him over countless jumps, he would probably still be grazing in Pine Hollow's meadow. Sure, his talent would eventually have been discovered, but the Macrae had given him his first opportunity. And he had handled it like a pro, just as they'd all thought he would.

Lisa realized that maybe she *had* given Samson an important start on a brilliant career. From now on, Red or someone of his caliber could continue Samson's lessons on the big show circuit. Lisa had no doubt that this was the first of many ribbons for the black horse.

AS HORSES AND riders continued to circle the ring, Lisa finally felt proud of herself. Riding in the Macrae, she realized, was one of the bravest and most difficult things she'd ever done.

Lisa noticed her mother sitting in the VIP box and clapping madly. "Good job, honey!" Mrs. Atwood called out, wiping her eyes. Lisa smiled fondly back and waved. Although her mother sometimes got caught up in the wrong things about riding, she had been really generous to buy Lisa that outfit. Even though the pink jacket had caused Lisa such embarrassment, it had still been a sweet thing to do.

Lisa noticed Jock Sawyer standing ringside with Kathy Colefield. She felt a thrill of recognition when she saw the two famous riders standing side by side. They were waving madly at someone, and out of curiosity, Lisa looked around to see who it was. Then with a shock she realized they were waving at her.

"Me?" she asked in disbelief, pointing at herself. Jock and Kathy laughed and nodded. "Congratulations!" they both called out. "That was a great performance!"

Lisa blushed, but she took it in stride. "Thanks!" she

called back. She leaned down to give Samson a pat. "I had a great horse!"

"Yeah, but I'd say he also had a great rider!" Jock called out.

A FEW MINUTES later the girls began untacking the horses and rubbing them down. Naturally, Veronica had vanished after her humiliation, leaving Danny to The Saddle Club. The day had been so exhilarating, however, that the girls didn't mind—and it wasn't as if it was the first time they'd looked after Veronica's horse!

"Listen," said Stevie after they had recapped the day's events several times, "I know you guys are pretty proud of yourselves. And you should be. But you do realize that a bigger challenge awaits?"

For a second Lisa's mind raced. Wasn't the competition over?

But Stevie was grinning mischievously. "The Grand Prix event is coming up soon," she said. "And I know exactly where I want to be to watch it—the VIP section!"

"Oh, no," said Carole, also grinning. "We don't have tickets for that."

"Exactly," Stevie said. "Who said anything about tickets? Let's sneak!"

Approximately ten minutes later, the girls sidled toward the box. "This is crazy!" wailed Lisa.

"Shhh," Stevie whispered. Then she stood up and nonchalantly eased into the box. She sat down in an empty seat and put her feet up on the seat in front of her as if she belonged there. "Nice horse," she said casually, gesturing toward the horse and rider in the ring.

Timidly Lisa and Carole followed Stevie's example, although with much less finesse and a lot more nervous giggling. "Look, there's your mother," said Carole, pointing toward Mrs. Atwood. Lisa hunched down in her seat and attempted to avoid being seen.

They had just settled down to watch the show when they heard a strident voice. "Those girls don't belong here!"

Turning, the girls saw Margie and Veronica sitting in the opposite corner of the box. Worse yet, Margie was standing up and pointing directly at them, glaring accusingly.

All around the girls, spectators shifted in their seats and turned to look at them. "Um, I'm starting to feel a bit conspicuous, aren't you?" mumbled Stevie.

"You said it," Carole breathed, trying not to look in Margie and Veronica's direction.

Margie and Veronica continued to protest The Saddle Club's presence in the box until finally a security person started to make his way over to the three girls.

Stevie was just getting ready to claim that she was the mayor's daughter—even though the mayor was sitting right there—when a voice interrupted Margie and Veronica with decisive firmness.

"Excuse me," it said. A few rows ahead, Jock Sawyer and Kathy Colefield stood up, turned around, and faced The Saddle Club and Margie and Veronica.

"Those girls," Jock said, pointing at Carole, Lisa, and Stevie, "are with us. We invited them to join us here. Kindly make room for them and allow them to enjoy the show, please."

"And please," added Kathy, giving Margie and Veronica a fierce glance, "kindly allow the rest of us to enjoy the show, too."

Margie and Veronica stopped their complaints immediately. Carole, Lisa, and Stevie gave each other high fives and settled back to watch the Grand Prix. At that moment, life was sweet.

13

"THE BEST PART about horse shows," said Stevie, "is going home."

She was sitting in the backseat of the van. The Pine Hollow group had been on the road for two hours. Traffic moved smoothly, and so far, there had been no flat tires.

"Oh, no," said Carole. "Horse shows are so much fun. Once you get over the fear," she added as an afterthought.

"But the ride home is great," insisted Stevie, reaching for another Oreo cookie. She had already eaten half a pack. The group had made a stop at a minimart and had loaded up on junk food for the ride home.

For the eighth time, the girls discussed the show. They talked about the horses they had seen, the riders they had met, and Samson and Starlight. Stevie and Carole showed Lisa the autographs they'd collected. Stevie had gotten some from people she didn't even know—and she couldn't read them. "I think this signature was from the guy running the concession stand," she said, pointing. "I didn't want to take a chance—he could've been a famous rider in disguise."

Most of all, they gloated over the look on Veronica's face when she had found out she'd been eliminated.

"What an ugly surprise that was," chuckled Stevie.

"If she hadn't been so busy preening for the judges, she might have done all right," Lisa said soberly.

"Nah," said Stevie. "I'm sure she would have found another way to mess it up. That," she finished, "was the crowning moment of the show for me. That made being tack manager completely worth it."

"You did a terrific job," came Max's voice from the driver's seat. "You can be my tack manager anytime."

"Not next time," warned Stevie, slumping back into the seat. "Next time I'll be on Belle."

"Hey, Max," said Carole. "Why was Jock Sawyer so interested in Samson? He sure asked a lot of questions about him."

Lisa finally got up the courage to ask the question on her mind, even though she was dreading the answer. "Is he interested in Samson for the USET?"

"Easy," said Max with a chuckle. "Jock was hinting that he would like to see Samson have a great career—

courtesy of him—but I pretty much pretended not to understand him. Samson's young yet. He can use a lot more training before he goes to the big leagues full-time. I don't plan to sell him for a while, so he's not going anywhere soon."

Lisa heaved a huge sigh of relief. She had become attached to Samson in their days of training for the Macrae, and she was glad he was going to be a part of Pine Hollow for a while. Max heard her sigh and glanced at her in the rearview mirror.

"Speaking of not going anywhere for a while," he said seriously, "I hope you stick to riding and training for big shows like the Macrae, Lisa. You did really well this weekend. I'm proud of your courage, and I'm proud that you climbed back on Samson after your fall and finished the course in such fine style."

Effusive praise from Max was rare. Lisa turned bright red and stammered her thanks.

Stevie, to save Lisa from her embarrassment, jumped into the conversation. "Say, Max, we heard a lot about you from Kathy Colefield," she teased. She was pleased to see the back of his neck turn red. "Guess we haven't heard a lot about the days before you became an old married man. Mrs. Reg told us you were a real heartbreaker!"

Max's neck turned even redder. But all he said was, "What about Mom before she met my father, Max the Second?"

"Huh?" the three girls said simultaneously in confusion.

"But Jock and I were just friends!" protested Mrs. Reg, but she, too, blushed and looked guilty.

"Honestly," said Stevie, pretending to be appalled, "I thought you guys were *horse*-crazy!"

ABOUT THE AUTHOR

Bonnie Bryant is the author of more than a hundred books about horses, including The Saddle Club series, Saddle Club Super Editions, and the Pony Tails series. She has also written novels and movie novelizations under her married name, B. B. Hiller.

Ms. Bryant began writing The Saddle Club in 1986. Although she had done some riding before that, she intensified her studies then and found herself learning right along with her characters Stevie, Carole, and Lisa. She claims that they are all much better riders than she is.

Ms. Bryant was born and raised in New York City. She still lives there, in Greenwich Village, with her two sons.

Don't miss the next exciting
Saddle Club adventure . . .

SIDESADDLE
Saddle Club #88

There's a new rider at Pine Hollow Stables. Her name is Tiffani. One member of The Saddle Club in particular is having a problem dealing with the newcomer. Carole Hanson and Lisa Atwood think Tiffani's a good rider, but Stevie Lake can't get over her riding gear—it's pink and covered in lace and frills. On top of that, Stevie just doesn't like Tiffani. It doesn't make sense, but she can't help it. When her boyfriend flirts with the new girl, Stevie stops seeing pink and starts seeing red. And when he praises Tiffani's riding skills, Stevie goes wild.

Suddenly she's in competition with Tiffani and determined to win at all costs—even if it means learning to jump fences while riding sidesaddle. Stevie's friends are convinced she's lost her mind. But Stevie's determined to "out-girl" Tiffani. She's even bought a fluffy pink sweater!